FLINT

Alpha Male Protector Romance and Suspense

A Guardian Hostage Rescue Specialists SHORT READ

ELLIE MASTERS
MASTER OF ROMANTIC SUSPENSE

JEM Publishing

Dedication

This book is dedicated to my one and only—my amazing and wonderful husband.

Without your care and support, my writing would not have made it this far.

You pushed me when I needed to be pushed.

You supported me when I felt discouraged.

You believed in me when I didn't believe in myself.

If it weren't for you, this book never would have come to life.

Also by Ellie Masters

The LIGHTER SIDE

Ellie Masters is the lighter side of the Jet & Ellie Masters writing duo! You will find Contemporary Romance, Military Romance, Romantic Suspense, Billionaire Romance, and Rock Star Romance in Ellie's Works.

YOU CAN FIND ELLIE'S BOOKS HERE:

ELLIEMASTERS.COM/BOOKS

Shop Ellie Masters Romantic Suspense and Steamy Contemporary Romance by series.

Angel Fire Rock Romance

Guardian HRS: Alpha Team

Guardian HRS: Bravo Team

Guardian HRS: Charlie Team

Guardian HRS: Delta Team

Cerberus Personal Security

The LaRouge Triplets

The One I Want Series

Angel's Peak Series

Billionaire Boy's Club

The Lovers

Changing Roles

SUGGESTED READING ORDER

START HERE

Rockstar Romance

The Angel Fire Rock Romance Series

EACH BOOK IN THIS SERIES CAN BE READ AS A STANDALONE AND IS ABOUT A DIFFERENT COUPLE WITH AN HEA.

IT IS RECOMMENDED THEY ARE READ IN ORDER.

Heart's Insanity

Ashes to New

Heart's Desire

Heart's Collide

Hearts Divided

Hearts Entwined

Forest's FALL

Hearts The Last Beat

CONTINUE HERE…

Military Romance

Guardian Hostage Rescue Specialists

Rescuing Melissa

(Get a FREE copy of Rescuing Melissa

when you join Ellie's Newsletter)

Alpha Team

Rescuing Zoe

Rescuing Moira

Rescuing Eve

Rescuing Lily

Rescuing Jinx

Rescuing Maria

Bravo Team

Brody

Cage

Billionaire Romance

Billionaire Boys Club

Hawke

Richard

Contemporary Romance

Cocky Captain

Romantic Suspense

EACH BOOK IS A STANDALONE NOVEL.

The Starling

The Swan

~AND~

Science Fiction

Ellie Masters writing as L.A. Warren
Vendel Rising: a Science Fiction Serialized Novel

If you enjoyed this book by Ellie Masters, the LIGHTER SIDE of the Jet & Ellie writing duo, and aren't afraid of edgier writing, you might enjoy reading BDSM themed books written by Jet, the DARKER SIDE of the Masters' Writing Team.

The DARKER SIDE

Jet Masters is the darker side of the Jet & Ellie writing duo!

Romantic Suspense

Changing Roles Series:

THIS SERIES MUST BE READ IN ORDER.

Command Me

Control Me

Collar Me

Embracing FATE

Seizing FATE

Accepting FATE

HOT READS

A STANDALONE NOVEL.

Down the Rabbit Hole

Light BDSM Romance

The Ties that Bind

EACH BOOK IN THIS SERIES CAN BE READ AS A STANDALONE AND IS ABOUT A DIFFERENT COUPLE WITH AN HEA.

Alexa

Penny

Michelle

Ivy

HOT READS

Becoming His Series

THIS SERIES MUST BE READ IN ORDER.

The Ballet

Learning to Breathe

Becoming His

Dark Captive Romance

A STANDALONE NOVEL.

She's MINE

This book is a work of fiction. It does not exist in the real world and should not be construed as reality. As in most romantic fiction, I've taken liberties. I've compressed the romance into a sliver of time. I've allowed these characters to develop strong bonds of trust over a matter of days.

This does not happen in real life where you, my amazing readers, live. Take more time in your romance and learn who you're giving a piece of your heart to. I urge you to move with caution. Always protect yourself.

Grab the First Book in The Guardian Hostage Rescue Specialists Series for Free

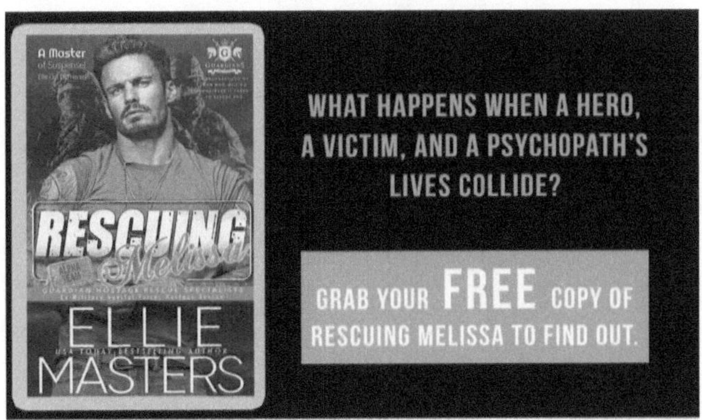

https://elliemasters.com/RescuingMelissa

ONE

FLINT

The California sun beats down on the Guardian HRS facility with the kind of intensity that makes asphalt shimmer and metal burn to the touch. I'm halfway across the compound, heading back from the range with cordite still sharp in my nostrils and the weight of my Glock familiar against my ribs, when my phone buzzes.

CJ's name on the screen. No message, just the summons I've learned to recognize after three years with Guardian HRS. Drop everything, come now, someone needs saving.

The paracord bracelet on my left wrist catches on my sleeve as I change direction, the worn green-and-tan weave rough under my fingers. I don't adjust it. Haven't taken it off in two years, not since the day I pulled it from the rubble in Kandahar and made promises to a dead man I couldn't keep. The weight of it reminds me what hesitation costs, what failure looks like when you're thirty seconds too late and the building's already come down.

I push through the main building's door into air conditioning that feels like a wall of ice after the heat outside. My boots are quiet on the polished concrete floors, the place designed with the kind of money that doesn't advertise itself but shows in every detail. Guardian HRS isn't flashy. We don't need to be. The people who need us know where to find us, and the people who should fear us learn quickly enough.

CJ's office is at the end of the north corridor, door half-open the way it always is when he's expecting someone. I knock anyway, two sharp raps, and push inside without waiting for an answer. He's at his desk, phone pressed to his ear, but he waves me in and points at the chair across from him. I take it, stretching my legs out and cataloging details while he finishes his conversation. There's a tablet on his desk displaying what looks like a bomb schematic, a physical file folder thick with papers, and two coffee cups that tell me he's been at this for a while. His jaw is tight, the muscle jumping in that way that means the situation is bad and getting worse.

He ends the call and tosses the phone onto his desk with enough force that it skitters across the surface. I wait. CJ doesn't waste time on small talk when something's burning, and whatever this is, it's definitely on fire.

"How fast can you get into the backcountry?" His eyes are sharp on mine, assessing. "Full pack, tracking scenario, rough terrain."

"Depends on the terrain. Give me six hours on anything in California." I lean forward, forearms on my knees. "What am I tracking?"

He slides the tablet across the desk toward me, and I catch it one-handed. The screen shows a personnel file, military record, and a photo that makes my breath catch for half a second before I lock it down.

The woman staring back at me has dark hair pulled into a braid, sharp hazel eyes that look like they don't miss much, and the kind of face that's more striking than pretty—strong jaw, straight nose, mouth that could smile or snarl with equal ease.

But it's something beyond the physical features that catches my eye, something in her expression that comes through even in a two-dimensional image.

Confidence. Intelligence.

A quiet strength that says she's been tested and didn't break.

Her eyes lock on mine, and everything in my body goes still— that recognition between predators, between survivors, between people who've walked through hell and come out breathing. She's beautiful in a way that hits me low and unexpected, dangerous in a way that makes my pulse kick up for reasons that have nothing to do with the mission.

I force myself to breathe, to catalog the response even as I shut it down.

This is a mission.

She's an asset who needs extraction and protection, not someone I should be noticing with this kind of intensity.

But my eyes keep returning to her face, to those hazel eyes that seem to look directly through the camera lens, and I'm aware of something shifting in my chest—recognition, maybe, or the beginning of something I don't have time to examine.

"Carolina Sutton," CJ says, and I drag my attention from her face to the text beside it. "Goes by Caro. Former Army EOD instructor, Fort Lee. Specialized in advanced trigger systems and counter-IED tactics. Honorably discharged three years ago after a training incident that killed one of her students."

I scan the details, absorbing them the way I've learned to process intel quickly and file it for later. She's thirty-two, grew up in Georgia, enlisted at eighteen, and went EOD after her first tour. Fast-tracked through instructor certification, earned commendations for innovation in device detection and disarmament.

Then the incident—a training exercise gone wrong, a student named Marcus Greer who got cocky and made a mistake that cost another soldier his life. The official investigation cleared her of wrongdoing, but reading between the lines of the report, I can see she didn't clear herself.

"She's been off the grid for nine days," CJ continues. "Works as a wilderness guide for a company based out of Santa Barbara, takes groups into Los Padres. Her boss says she requested personal time and went solo into the backcountry. He doesn't know exactly where, just that she does this every year around this time."

"Anniversary of the training death," I say, connecting the dots. The date in the file matches up. She's out there processing, punishing herself with isolation the way some people do when guilt won't let them rest. I know the impulse. I've been wearing it on my wrist for two years.

"Yeah." CJ pulls the tablet back and swipes to a different file. "Here's why we need her. Forty-eight hours ago, the FBI arrested Marcus Greer—the same student from her training incident—attempting to place an explosive device at a water treatment facility outside Los Angeles. They disarmed it, started interrogating him, and he gave them just enough to realize he's got more devices out there. Plural. One already detonated at a remote electrical substation yesterday morning. Minimal casualties, but it's escalating."

My jaw tightens. "He's targeting infrastructure."

"That's what the FBI thinks, but it's worse than that." CJ's expression goes even grimmer. "The devices use a trigger system Sutton designed. Highly sophisticated, adaptive, and nearly impossible to disarm using standard protocols. FBI's best techs are stumped. They brought in ATF, consulted with Army EOD, and everyone keeps coming back to the same conclusion—they need the person who invented it."

"And Greer's talking in riddles," I guess, because that's how these things always go. The bomber who wants an audience, who has a point to prove.

"Exactly. He's dropping hints about the next device, but only someone who knows him personally would recognize the references. The FBI thinks this is personal for him. He's not just attacking infrastructure—he's attacking her." CJ meets my eyes. "They think he's trying to draw her out, make her face what her design can do in the wrong hands. Prove she was always dangerous."

I look at the photo again, at those hazel eyes that have seen too much. She went into the wilderness to process her guilt, and now the past is coming for her whether she's ready or not. The irony would be bitter if it weren't so damn predictable. You can't outrun what haunts you. I learned that the hard way.

"Timeline?" I ask, already running calculations in my head. Los Padres is big, thousands of acres of rugged terrain. If she's been off-grid for nine days and her boss doesn't know her exact location, finding her is going to take skill and time we might not have.

"Device three is estimated to activate in approximately twenty-two hours based on Greer's pattern. Could be less. FBI's working on narrowing down the location from his clues, but they need Sutton's expertise to disarm it." CJ stands, moving to the map of California mounted on his wall. He taps the area around Los Padres National Forest. "Her company says she usually works in this region. Her vehicle's been parked at the Alameda Trailhead for eight days. Rangers confirm they haven't seen her, but that's not unusual—she knows the backcountry and tends to avoid the main trails."

I study the map, the vast green expanse that could hide someone who doesn't want to be found. Eight days is a long time to be alone out there. She'll have established a pattern, found water sources, and set up camps in defensible positions if she's got any tactical sense. And based on her file, she's got plenty.

"You want me to find her and bring her in." It's not a question.

"You've got SERE training, you've tracked HVTs through worse terrain than this, and you're the best tracker on the team." CJ turns from the map. "I need her found fast, Flint. And I need her willing to help. She's been out of the game for three years, probably dealing with PTSD from the training incident. You're going to have to convince her to face the exact thing she's been running from."

I think about the bracelet on my wrist, about the weight of guilt and how it shapes everything you do afterward. About how hard it is to trust yourself again when you've failed someone who counted on you. I might be the right person for this job, but not for the reasons CJ thinks.

"I'll find her," I say, standing. "Twenty-two hours gives me time if I move fast."

"Helicopter's being prepped now. You'll have a satellite phone, an emergency beacon, and full briefing materials on Greer and the devices." CJ hands me the file folder from his desk. "Read this on the flight. And Flint—she's going to be resistant. She left this world behind for a reason."

I tuck the folder under my arm and head for the door, but his voice stops me before I clear the threshold.

"One more thing. The FBI has reason to believe Greer had help with the devices. At least one partner, possibly more. If he knows where Sutton is—and he might, given how obsessed he seems to be—they could already be looking for her."

The implications settle into my gut like lead. I'm not just tracking her. I might be racing someone else to find her first, and that someone wants her dead or captured for leverage. The timeline just got tighter.

"Understood," I say, and let the door close behind me.

Twenty minutes later, I'm in a helicopter, pack secured between my boots and the file folder open on my lap. The pilot lifts us into the air, and the facility drops away beneath us as we bank toward the mountains. I can see the coastline from here, the Pacific stretching endlessly blue, and inland the green-brown expanse of Los Padres rising into ridges and canyons that could swallow a person whole.

I open the folder and start reading, committing details to memory the way I've done a hundred times before on mission prep. Marcus Greer, thirty-four, a former Army EOD specialist, was dishonorably discharged after the training incident that killed Private Noah Parker.

Greer blamed Sutton for designing a device that was too realistic, too dangerous for training purposes. She blamed him for arrogance and failure to follow protocol. The investigation sided with her, but Greer's career was over either way. He went dark after discharge, dropped off the radar for two years, and resurfaced six months ago in Los Angeles, working construction. FBI thinks he spent the missing time radicalizing, building connections, and planning this.

The device schematics are complex, elegant in a way that makes it clear Sutton knows her craft. The trigger system is adaptive—it learns from disarmament attempts and adjusts its parameters to counter them.

It's brilliant and terrifying, the kind of innovation that saves lives when used for training but becomes a nightmare in the wrong hands. Reading her design notes, I can see the mind behind it: precise, creative, always three steps ahead. She thought through every angle, anticipated every approach. That same mind is now the only thing standing between Greer's devices and mass casualties.

There are photos of her in the file beyond the personnel shot. One from Afghanistan, standing with her unit in dusty fatigues, that slight smile playing at her mouth. One from her teaching days, demonstrating something to a group of students, her hands moving as she explains. One more recent, maybe a year old, from the wilderness guide company's website. She's in hiking gear, standing on a ridge with mountains behind her, and the smile is gone. Her eyes look distant, haunted by things she can't leave behind.

I close the folder and look out the window at the terrain passing beneath us. The helicopter follows Highway 101 north before cutting inland toward the mountains. The landscape shifts from coastal scrub to oak woodland to the denser vegetation of the higher elevations. Los Padres is a patchwork of ecosystems, from chaparral-covered hills to pine forests to rocky canyons where water carves through limestone and sandstone. Good country for someone who wants to disappear.

The pilot's voice crackles through my headset. "Five minutes to LZ."

TWO

FLINT

I CHECK MY GEAR ONE MORE TIME, RUNNING THROUGH THE MENTAL list. Glock 19 on my hip, Ka-Bar knife strapped to my thigh, satellite phone and emergency beacon in waterproof pouches, first aid kit, water filtration system, three days of rations, bivvy sack, and the portable tablet with her file loaded.

I'm dressed for speed and flexibility—lightweight hiking boots broken in years ago, cargo pants with reinforced knees, a moisture-wicking shirt under a tactical vest that carries extra magazines and supplies. The paracord bracelet catches my eye as I adjust my pack straps, and I run my thumb over it once before forcing my attention back to the mission.

The helicopter descends toward a clearing near the Alameda Trailhead, and I can see a small parking area with a handful of vehicles below. One of them will be hers—the file said a dark green Jeep Wrangler, seven years old, well-maintained. The kind of vehicle that says she values reliability over flash.

We touch down with barely a bump, and I'm out the door before the skids fully settle, pack on my shoulders, and head down against the rotor wash. The pilot gives me a thumbs-up through the windscreen, and then the helicopter is lifting away, leaving me in sudden silence broken only by wind through pine trees and the distant call of a hawk.

The parking area is deserted except for the vehicles. I find the Jeep easily—it's the only one that looks like it's been here for days, with a fine layer of dust coating the windshield and pine needles accumulated on the hood.

I peer through the windows without touching anything. The interior is clean and organized, and a first-aid kit is visible in the back seat, along with a climbing rope and a duffel bag. Nothing screams distress or hurried departure. She planned this trip, packed deliberately, and walked into the wilderness with purpose.

I head to the trailhead kiosk where hikers are supposed to sign in, but there's no log entry from her. Not surprising—she knows this area too well to bother with official channels, and if she wanted privacy, advertising her route would defeat the purpose. I study the trail map posted behind scratched plexiglass, noting the main arteries that branch into smaller paths, the elevation markers, and the water sources.

If I were her, wanting solitude and processing space, where would I go?

High.

Away from the popular trails. Somewhere with good sight lines and access to water. Defensible if she's thinking tactically, which her training suggests she would be, even subconsciously.

I find the ranger station a quarter mile down the access road, a small wooden building with solar panels on the roof and a weather-beaten sign. A ranger in his fifties looks up from his desk when I walk in, taking in my appearance with the practiced assessment of someone who deals with all kinds coming through these mountains.

"Help you?" His voice is friendly but cautious.

"I'm looking for someone who might have come through here about eight, nine days ago." I pull out my phone and show him Caro's photo, the one from her guide company website. "Carolina Sutton. She's a wilderness guide, experienced, would have been going solo."

His expression shifts to recognition. "Yeah, I know Caro.

Haven't seen her this trip, but she comes through a few times a year. Keeps to herself mostly." His eyes narrow slightly. "She in some kind of trouble?"

"She's needed for an emergency consultation," I say, which is true enough. "Time-sensitive. Her company said she went into the backcountry, but didn't specify where. Any idea where she might head?"

He chews his lip, weighing how much to tell me. "You a friend of hers?"

"No. But she's not in trouble—she's the solution to someone else's trouble. I just need to find her quickly." I meet his eyes, letting him see I'm serious. "People's lives depend on it."

Something in my tone convinces him. He moves to a large topographical map on the wall, studying it for a moment before tapping a section of high country northeast of our location.

"If she wanted real solitude, she'd head up here. Good water from snowmelt, even this time of year, far away from the main trails, plenty of terrain variety. She mentioned once that she likes the ridge systems up there—you can see for miles, watch the sunrise and sunset from the same spot."

I commit the area to memory, noting the elevations and approaches. "How long to get up there?"

"For most people? Ten, twelve hours with a full pack. For Caro?" He shrugs. "She'd do it in eight. And that's assuming she took the standard route. She knows shortcuts most folks don't."

I thank him and head back to the trailhead, using the tablet to pull up detailed topographical maps of the region he indicated. The terrain is steep, rising from around three thousand feet here to over six thousand in the high country. I plot the most likely approach routes, taking into account water sources and camping locations. She's been out here nine days. That's long enough to settle in, to establish patterns. If I can find her first camp, I can track her movement from there.

I check my watch. The sun is high and hot, and I've got maybe eight hours of good daylight left. I need to move fast but not recklessly. Missing signs because I'm hurrying would cost me more time than I'd save.

I shoulder my pack and start up the trail at a ground-eating pace that I can maintain for hours. The path is well-worn at first, wide enough for two people, but within a mile it narrows and steepens. I push through manzanita and oak, watching for anything that doesn't belong—a broken branch, a boot print, a disturbance in the natural pattern of the forest. The temperature drops as I gain elevation, and the vegetation shifts to more pine and fir, the air sharp with resin and the loamy smell of decomposing needles.

After two hours, I find the first sign. A boot print in soft dirt near a creek crossing, partial but clear enough. Women's size eight or nine, tread pattern from a high-quality hiking boot. The edges are softened by weather, days old. I kneel beside it, examining the depth and angle. She crossed here heading northeast, moving with confidence. No hesitation in the stride length.

I follow the creek upstream, knowing water is the magnet that draws everything in the wilderness. Another hour and I find her first camp in a small clearing sheltered by granite boulders and overlooking a narrow valley. The site is clean—she packed out everything she brought in—but the signs are there for someone who knows how to look. Disturbed pine needles where her tent was pitched, a ring of stones around a long-cold fire pit, a spot where she clearly sat for long periods based on the compressed earth and the way the grass hasn't fully rebounded.

I circle the camp slowly, reading the story it tells. She stayed here at least two nights, maybe three. Did minimal cooking, kept the fire small and controlled. There's a spot where she must have sat watching the sunset, the western view open and spectacular from this vantage. I can picture her there, knees drawn up, processing whatever demons drove her into these mountains.

But she didn't stay. Something made her move deeper, higher, farther from the world. I find the direction she left, heading northeast again toward even more remote country. The trail she followed—if you can call it a trail—is barely visible, more of a game path than anything humans made. She's not just hiking. She's hiding.

That realization shifts something in my chest. I scan the surrounding terrain more carefully, looking for signs of anyone else passing through. The ranger mentioned she comes here regularly. If Greer or his people know her patterns, they could have found her vehicle the same way I did. They could be ahead of me right now.

I pick up my pace, following her track through increasingly rugged country. She's good—better than good.

Twice, I lose the trail and have to backtrack, casting in widening circles until I find the next sign. A scuff mark on a rock face where she climbed. A bent twig that's trying to spring back but hasn't quite. She's covering her tracks without making it obvious, the kind of tradecraft that comes from military training and paranoia earned the hard way.

The sun is sinking toward the western ridges when I find evidence that confirms my suspicion. Boot prints that aren't hers, fresher than her trail, moving parallel to her direction. Men's size eleven, two different individuals based on the tread patterns. They're tracking her, and they're twelve hours behind where she is now, but only a few hours ahead of me.

My hand drops to my Glock, thumb checking the retention strap. The mission just shifted from search and rescue to something more complicated. I need to find her before they do, and I need to do it without tipping them off that I'm here.

I move faster, taking calculated risks to make up time. The terrain is steep and unforgiving, loose scree that wants to slide underfoot, granite faces that require scrambling, dense patches of manzanita that tear at clothing and skin. My legs burn with the sustained effort, and sweat soaks through my shirt despite the cooling air. The paracord bracelet chafes against my wrist where my pack strap rubs it, a constant reminder of what failure costs.

Not this time. Not her.

The sun is still high but beginning its descent toward the western ridges, the light turning golden when I crest a ridge.

I pull out binoculars and scan carefully, looking for movement, and finally catch a glimpse of her. She's sitting on a rock outcropping, silhouetted against the dying light, and even from this distance,

I can see the weapon held in lap. She's watching the approaches, alert despite days of solitude.

Professional. Capable. Exactly what her file suggested she'd be.

I adjust the binoculars, bringing her into sharper focus, and something in my chest tightens.

Even from this distance, something is compelling about the way she holds herself—spine straight, shoulders back. I track the line of her throat, the way her braid falls over one shoulder.

This is a problem.

I'm supposed to be assessing her as a tactical asset —a subject who needs extraction —not noticing the graceful curve of her neck or the way the fading light turns her profile into something almost artistic.

I lower the binoculars and scrub a hand over my face, forcing myself to refocus.

Mission first. Always mission first. The unwanted awareness of her as a woman—as someone attractive—is just biology, adrenaline, the isolation of being alone in the wilderness. It doesn't mean anything. It won't affect my performance.

I raise the binoculars again, and immediately my eyes find her. Yeah. This might be more complicated than I anticipated.

I keep thinking about the way she held herself, rifle across her lap, watching the approaches with the kind of alertness that comes from training and experience. Professional, capable, and completely unaware of being observed.

I wonder what she's thinking right now, alone in her bivvy. Whether she's processing the anniversary that drove her out here, or if she's finally finding some peace. Whether she's as ready to face what's waiting below as she needs to be.

The paracord bracelet on my wrist catches moonlight, and I run my thumb over it absently. Tomorrow I'll walk into her camp and ask her to face her worst nightmare. Ask her to trust me—a stranger —to keep her alive while she disarms devices designed specifically to kill her. It's a lot to ask of anyone, let alone someone who's spent nine days in isolation trying to escape her demons.

But watching her earlier, seeing the competence and strength in every movement, I think she can handle it. More than that—I think she needs to handle it. Needs to prove to herself that she's more than her failures, more than her guilt.

I just have to make sure she survives long enough to realize it.

My mind drifts, unbidden, to the photo in her file. Those hazel eyes, that strong jaw, the confidence in her expression. She's even more compelling in person—real and three-dimensional in a way no photograph can capture. The way she moves, the intelligence behind her eyes when she assessed the threat I represented, the controlled tension in her body language that speaks to someone who's always ready, always aware.

I shake my head, annoyed at myself. This is tactical assessment, nothing more. Doesn't matter that she's attractive or that something about her presence has been pulling at me since I first saw her through the binoculars.

I'm here on a mission to extract her, keep her safe, until she can do her job. Simple. Professional.

I consider my approach. She'll hear me coming, and I'll have a weapon pointed at me before I can explain. Better to come in with my hands visible and hope she's willing to listen before she shoots.

I'll use her name, identify Guardian HRS, and show her credentials before I get too close. The photo of Greer and the device schematics should be enough to get her attention, and then I have to convince her that people need her more than she needs this isolation.

Simple.

Except nothing about this is simple. She's out here because she couldn't face what her design did in the wrong hands the first time. Now I'm going to ask her to face it again, under even higher stakes, with even less time to prepare.

I touch the bracelet on my wrist, feeling the familiar texture of the weave. I know what it's like to carry guilt that won't let go. I know what it's like to question every decision you've ever made because one of them got someone killed. And I know what it's like when the world demands you step back into the fire anyway because you're the only one who can.

THREE

CAROLINA

THE AFTERNOON SHADOWS LENGTHEN ACROSS THE CANYON AS I SIT on my favorite rock outcropping, rifle across my lap, watching the approaches the way I have every day since arriving.

Nine days. I've been out here nine days, and it still doesn't feel like enough distance from the date circled in red on every calendar I've ever owned since it happened.

Three years ago today, Private Noah Parker bled out on a training field at Fort Lee while I screamed at the medics to work faster and Marcus Greer stood with his hands shaking and his face white with shock. Three years, and I can still smell the copper tang of blood mixing with Virginia clay, still hear the wet sound of Noah trying to breathe around the shrapnel that had torn through his chest because Greer got cocky.

I stand before the memories drag me deeper. Movement helps. Action helps. Sitting still lets the past catch up, and I didn't come out here to drown in it—I came to make peace with it, or at least to stop fighting the parts I can't change.

The air is that thin mountain cold that comes with elevation and clear skies. The sun sets and the golden hour begins, promising a spectacular sunset.

I left my tent behind this time, bringing only the lightweight bivvy sack that keeps the dew off and weighs almost nothing. The less I carry, the farther I can go, and I need to go far this year.

Need to find a place where even the echoes of civilization can't reach me.

I do a slow scan of my surroundings, hand loose on my weapon's grip, checking the approaches and sight lines the way I've done every day since I got here.

Old habits. Army habits. EOD habits that say you always clear the area, always check for threats, always assume someone might want you dead, because sometimes they do.

The canyon is empty except for me and the resident ravens. One of them croaks from a pine tree twenty yards away, watching me with that unsettling intelligence corvids have. I've been feeding it scraps, and now it expects breakfast like I'm running a goddamn diner up here.

My camp is minimal—the bivvy sack rolled tight and secured to my pack, fire ring from last night's small blaze now just gray ash and cold stones, water bottles lined up beside my pack where I filled them from the spring last night.

Everything has its place, everything is organized the way the Army taught me, and EOD reinforced. When you work with explosives for a living, disorder isn't just inconvenient—it's deadly. A misplaced tool, a forgotten step, a moment of inattention, and people die.

Like Noah.

I shake off the thought and move to the fire ring, building a new fire from tinder and kindling for tonight's meal. The motions are mechanical, soothing in their simplicity. Scrape a nest in the ash, place the tinder, arrange the kindling in a teepee, light one match — because I'm not wasting resources —and breathe gently to encourage the flame.

Smoke rises thin and pale, and I feed it carefully until the fire is self-sustaining. Coffee first, then food, then decide whether to stay another day or push higher into the backcountry.

Except I know the answer already. I'm leaving tomorrow.

Nine days is enough.

The anniversary has passed, Noah's ghost is no quieter, but at least I've paid my respects with solitude and guilt, and I need to get back before my boss at Sierra Wilderness Expeditions starts to worry. I texted him from the trailhead before I lost signal that I'd be out for a week, maybe ten days, and he knows I do this every year. But there's a limit to how long you can disappear before people start asking questions I don't want to answer.

The coffee is instant, tastes like dirt and chemicals, and I drink it black while watching the sun set over the western ridges. Light spills into the canyon in shades of gold and amber, painting the granite faces and turning the pine needles to bronze. It's beautiful in a way that makes my chest ache.

Out here, nothing explodes.

Nothing bleeds.

Nothing dies because I made a mistake in judgment three years ago when I thought training devices could simulate real-world threats without real-world consequences.

I'm finishing the coffee when the raven goes silent. One moment it's muttering to itself in that conversational way ravens have, and the next it's gone completely quiet. I set the cup down slowly and reach for the Sig, thumbing off the safety as I scan the tree line. Birds don't shut up without reason.

Something's coming.

I move to a position behind the rocks that form the natural wall of my camp, sighting along the most likely approaches. My heart rate picks up but stays controlled—adrenaline without panic, the way I learned to manage it when a wrong move could set off an IED.

Breathe. Focus. Assess.

It takes me three minutes to spot him. He's good, I'll give him that. Moving carefully through the scrub oak and manzanita, using cover, keeping noise to a minimum. But I've been staring at this terrain for nine days, and I know what belongs and what doesn't.

He's coming from the southwest, uphill, which is smart—it gives him the high ground advantage and makes him harder to spot against the setting sun. He's big, broad-shouldered, moving with the kind of controlled grace that says military or law enforcement. Tactical pants, hiking boots, and a pack that's neither too heavy nor too light. Armed—I can see the pistol on his hip from here.

My finger rests alongside the trigger guard, not on the trigger. Not yet. He hasn't done anything overtly threatening, but he's also not a hiker who stumbled onto my camp by accident.

Nobody comes up here by accident.

This is deliberate.

I wait until he's forty yards out.

"That's close enough." My voice cuts through the quiet, sharp and clear. I keep the Sig pointed at him but not quite aimed—a warning, not an execution.

He freezes immediately, hands coming away from his sides, palms visible.

Smart.

Non-threatening but not submissive.

His head turns slowly toward me, and I get my first clear look at his face. Strong features, maybe mid-thirties, dark hair cut military-short, eyes that are either gray or blue—hard to tell from this distance. There's a hardness to him, the kind that comes from seeing and doing things that change you, but also something else.

Something steady.

Something that catches me off-guard.

He's handsome in a way that's all angles and rough edges, nothing soft or pretty about it. Square jaw dark with stubble, straight nose that looks like it's been broken at least once, mouth set in a firm line that somehow still manages to look... appealing.

The tactical gear emphasizes broad shoulders and a trim waist, the kind of build that comes from functional strength rather than vanity.

My pulse kicks up, and I tell myself it's just adrenaline, just the surprise of being found after nine days alone. It has nothing to do with the way he holds himself—controlled power, competence written into every line of his body—or the steady intelligence in his eyes as he assesses the situation without a hint of panic.

I tighten my grip on the Sig, annoyed at myself. This is not the time to notice that a man is attractive.

This is the time to figure out if he's a threat and what he wants.

Focus, Sutton.

"Carolina Sutton?" His voice is calm, pitched to carry without shouting. No panic, no aggression. Just steady, like his eyes.

The fact that he knows my name makes my finger move fractionally closer to the trigger. "Who's asking?"

"My name is Flint Morrison. I'm with Guardian HRS." He moves one hand very slowly toward his vest, two fingers only. "I'm reaching for credentials. Don't shoot me."

Guardian HRS. The name triggers recognition—private security, former military operators, the kind of people who get called when situations are too sensitive or too complicated for standard law enforcement.

I don't lower the weapon, but I don't tell him to stop either. He pulls out a slim wallet and holds it up, letting me see the ID and badge before tossing it gently toward me. It lands in the dirt ten feet away.

"Stay there," I tell him, and move to retrieve it without taking my eyes or the gun off him. I crouch, pick up the wallet one-handed, and flip it open. The ID looks legitimate—his photo, the Guardian HRS logo. Could be fake, but it would be a good fake.

I toss it back to him. "Guardian HRS doesn't make social calls. What do you want?"

"I need you to come with me. There's a situation that requires your expertise." He hasn't moved from where I stopped him, hands still visible, body language open. "Time-sensitive. Lives at stake."

"I'm on leave." I adjust my stance slightly, keeping the rock outcropping between us. "Whatever it is, FBI or ATF or Army EOD can handle it. I'm not in that world anymore."

"It's not that simple." He takes a slow breath, deciding how much to tell me. "Marcus Greer is in FBI custody. He's been placing explosive devices across California using a trigger system you designed. One's already detonated. At least two more are active. FBI's techs can't disarm them. They need you."

The name hits me like a fist to the solar plexus. Marcus Greer. The last person I want to think about, connected to the last thing I want to touch. My hand doesn't waver on the gun, but something in my chest clenches tight.

"Greer?" My voice sounds flat even to my own ears. Dishonorable discharge. He blamed me for his failure.

Morrison's eyes are sharp on mine, reading my reaction. "He spent the last three years planning this. The devices use your adaptive trigger design. He's modified them, made them more lethal. And he's talking in riddles during interrogation, dropping hints about the next target that only someone who knows him would understand." He pauses. "They think this is about you, Ms. Sutton. He's trying to prove something, or draw you out, or both."

I want to tell him he's wrong. I want to send him back down the mountain and pretend this conversation never happened. But the tactical part of my brain—the part that kept me alive through two deployments and three years teaching people how not to die—is already processing the information, and it makes too much sense.

Greer always was obsessed with proving himself, with being the best, with showing everyone who doubted him that he was smarter than they gave him credit for. And he blamed me for ruining his career, even though he ruined it himself by being arrogant and careless.

"If he's in custody, why do you need me?" I'm stalling, and we both know it.

"Because he's not giving up the locations easily, and even if he did, the FBI can't disarm devices built using your design. You invented it. You know how it thinks, how it adapts." Morrison takes a small step forward, testing my boundaries. "Every minute we waste is a minute closer to people dying."

The sun is slipping down toward the horizon, but is still warm on my shoulders. There's something in his expression beyond the professional urgency—concern, maybe, or recognition. Like he knows what he's asking of me, knows how much I don't want to do this, and understands why.

His right wrist has a paracord bracelet wrapped around it, worn and faded, the kind of thing soldiers make or carry for luck or memory. There's a story there, probably one as ugly as mine.

I lower the Sig slightly, safety back on, and tuck it into the holster at my hip. "Show me what you have."

FOUR

CAROLINA

HE MOVES FORWARD CAREFULLY, REACHING INTO HIS PACK AND pulling out a tablet wrapped in a protective case. When he's fifteen feet away, I stop him again, and he sets it on a flat rock before backing off. I move forward to collect it, hyperaware of his presence —the way he holds himself, the economy of movement, the fact that he's armed but hasn't touched his weapon once since showing his hands empty.

Professional. Respectful.

But also... I notice details I shouldn't. The breadth of his shoulders under the tactical shirt, the strong lines of his face, the way his eyes track me without being aggressive about it.

I shake off the awareness and focus on the tablet. He's already unlocked it, pulled up files. I scroll through quickly, absorbing information the way I was trained to—fast, thorough, no emotional attachment to what I'm reading.

There are crime scene photos of Device One at the water treatment facility. My breath catches when I see it. That's my design, no question. The housing, the trigger mechanism, and the redundancy protocols I built in to make it challenging but not impossible for advanced students to disarm.

But there are modifications—additional components I don't recognize, bypass systems that look like they're designed to kill anyone using my standard teaching methods.

He's weaponized my training tool. Made it into something that would murder the very people I taught to stay alive.

I scroll to the photos of Device Two, the one that detonated. The aftermath is ugly—twisted metal, scorched earth, and structural damage to the electrical substation. The report says minimal casualties, but minimal doesn't mean none.

Someone died because Greer used my design to kill them.

"There's more," Morrison says quietly. He moved closer without me noticing, standing ten feet away now. "The interrogation transcripts."

He closes the distance to maybe six feet, and I'm suddenly aware of the space between us—or the lack of it. He's taller than I realized, at least eight, maybe ten, inches on me, and the morning sun backlights him, emphasizing the breadth of his shoulders.

I catch his scent—sweat and pine and something clean, masculine, that cuts through the mountain air.

When he leans in to point at something on the tablet screen, his shoulder nearly brushes mine, and I feel the heat radiating off him. For a man who just hiked deep into the wilderness to find me, he smells surprisingly good, and I'm annoyed at myself for noticing.

"Here," he says, tapping the screen, and his voice is lower, rougher than before.

Close enough that I feel the vibration of it.

I force myself to focus on the words, not on the man standing so close I could reach out and touch him. Not on the way my body wants to lean into that warmth, that solid presence.

This is tactical information. Lives at stake. Not the time to be distracted by broad shoulders and steady gray eyes.

But my hands aren't entirely steady when I take the tablet from him, and when our fingers brush in the exchange, the contact sends an unexpected jolt through me that has nothing to do with static electricity.

I pull up the file and start reading. Greer's words jump off the screen, smug and cryptic. *"The Girl Scout always comes prepared, but did she prepare for this?"*

Girl Scout.

That was his nickname for me back at Fort Lee, said with just enough edge to make it an insult disguised as affection. I was always prepared, always had backup plans, always thought three steps ahead. He resented it even as he pretended to admire it.

"Where Girl Scouts earn their badges," I read aloud from another line. My mind immediately supplies context—Camp Cielo Azul, a wilderness education center in the Los Padres foothills where I used to volunteer teaching orienteering and wilderness survival to youth groups. I spent dozens of weekends there, and Greer knew about it because he made jokes about me wasting my time with kids when I could be doing something more important.

"You recognize the reference," Morrison says. It's not a question.

"Yeah." My voice is rough. "He's pointing to a location. A place he knows I'd identify." I look up from the tablet to meet his eyes. "This is targeted. Specifically at me. He wants me to come, wants me to try to disarm his devices, probably wants me to fail so he can prove I was always dangerous."

"Or he wants you dead." Morrison's expression is grim. "FBI thinks he might have a partner still active. Someone is placing devices while he's in custody. Someone who might have orders to take you out if you show up."

The morning suddenly feels colder, despite the sun. I hand the tablet back to him, and our fingers brush in the exchange—rough calluses, warm skin, the brief contact sending an unexpected jolt of awareness through me. I pull back quickly, annoyed at myself. Not the time. Not remotely the time.

"How did you find me?" I ask, buying myself a moment to think.

"Tracked you. Your company said you were out here somewhere. I started at the trailhead where your Jeep's parked, followed your trail." He slides the tablet back into his pack. "You're good, but I'm better at tracking than most people are at hiding."

There's no arrogance in the statement, just fact. And he's right

—I didn't expect to be found. Didn't think anyone would be looking. "Anyone else looking for me?"

His jaw tightens. "Maybe. I found boot prints yesterday that weren't yours and weren't mine. Two people, moving parallel to your route. Could be hikers. Could be something else."

The implications settle cold in my stomach. If Greer told his partner where I might be, they could have been searching while I was processing anniversary guilt up here in the wilderness. They could be close right now.

I look around at my camp, at the peace I've tried to carve out of solitude and distance.

Nine days isn't enough.

Will never be enough.

Because the past doesn't stay buried just because you run from it —it follows you, finds you, demands payment in blood and guilt and the one thing you swore you'd never do again.

But if I don't go, people die. Children, maybe, if Device Three is where I think it is. Innocent people who had nothing to do with my failure three years ago are now caught in the blast radius of Greer's revenge.

I meet Morrison's eyes. He's watching me, patient but urgent, and there's something in his expression that makes me think he understands the weight of this decision. The paracord bracelet on his wrist catches the light, and I wonder what promise or failure he's carrying, what ghost drives him the way Noah's drives me.

"How long do I have?" My voice is steadier than I feel.

"Twelve hours. Maybe less." He pauses. "I have a helicopter waiting at the trailhead. We can be at Guardian HQ in two hours, the FBI briefing room an hour after that."

Twelve hours to stop a device I designed from killing people, using knowledge that got someone killed three years ago. Twelve hours to face Marcus Greer's revenge and prove that I'm not the monster he wants me to be—or that I am.

I think of Noah, young and eager and dead, because I thought I could make training realistic without making it lethal. I think of the unknown people who will die if Device Three detonates, their families, their futures erased because I don't have the courage to face my past.

"I need five minutes to break camp." I move toward my bivvy sack, already making decisions about what to pack, what to leave. "We'll move fast getting down. If there are people looking for me, I'd rather not make it easy for them."

Before I can move away, his hand catches my wrist—not restraining, just... connecting. The touch stops me mid-step.

When I look up, his eyes are on mine, storm-gray and intense, and for a breath the mountain falls away. There's heat there, unmistakable, and something else—recognition, maybe, like he's seeing past my walls to the woman underneath.

I should pull away. Should maintain distance, professionalism, all the walls I've built.

But I don't.

For three heartbeats, we stand there, close enough that I can feel the warmth radiating off him, can see the flecks of darker gray in his eyes, can feel my pulse kick up in response to whatever this reaction might be.

Then he releases me, stepping back, and the mountain rushes back in around us—cold air, pine scent, the mission waiting below.

"Five minutes," he says, voice rougher than before. "Agreed." Morrison unslings his pack and pulls out a radio. "I'll call for the helicopter, have them ready to go the second we hit the trailhead."

I roll up the bivvy, everything finding its place in my pack through muscle memory that doesn't need conscious thought. Freeze-dried food, water filtration system, first aid kit, rope, knife, fire starter, and spare clothing. The Sig goes into a holster that clips to my pack's hip belt for easy access. Everything else gets left—the fire ring, the memories, the attempt at peace that failed before it started.

Morrison is talking quietly into his radio, confirming extraction and updating someone named CJ on the situation. I catch fragments: "Subject located... cooperative... possible hostile surveillance... ETA two hours."

Subject. That's me.

Back in the world where I'm not Caro, who guides hikers through beautiful country, but Carolina Sutton, who designs devices that kill and might be able to stop someone from doing it again.

I shoulder my pack, the weight familiar and grounding. Morrison ends his call and turns to me, and for a moment we just look at each other. Two people shaped by violence and carrying ghosts, about to walk into more violence together. There's an understanding in his eyes that I wasn't expecting, something that says he knows the cost of what he's asking and respects that I'm paying it anyway.

"Ready?" he asks.

No. I'll never be ready. But being ready doesn't matter when the clock is ticking.

"Yeah." I do a final scan of the camp, making sure I haven't left anything that matters. The raven is back in its tree, watching us with those intelligent eyes. "Let's move. Stay sharp—if Greer knows where I go, his people might have found my camp the same way you did."

Morrison's expression sharpens, hand dropping casually closer to his weapon. "You take point. You know this terrain better than I do. I'll watch our six."

It's the right call, trusting my expertise in my domain, and I respect him for making it without ego. I start down the trail at a pace that's fast but sustainable, picking the route that gives us cover and good sight lines. Behind me, Morrison moves quietly for someone his size, and I can feel his presence like a physical thing—protective without being oppressive, alert without radiating paranoia.

The sun climbs higher as we descend, heat building despite the elevation. Sweat soaks into my shirt, and my legs settle into the rhythm of long-distance hiking that I can maintain for hours. My mind tries to wander toward what's waiting at the bottom of this mountain—FBI briefings, device schematics, Greer's smug face in some interrogation room—but I force it back to the present.

Watch the trail. Check the surroundings. Stay alive long enough to deal with the rest.

We're maybe forty minutes into the descent when Morrison's voice comes low from behind me. "Stop."

I freeze mid-step, hand moving toward the Sig. "What?"

"Broken branch at ten o'clock. Fresh. Not from wildlife." His voice is barely above a whisper. "Someone came through here recently. Moving fast."

I see it now—the branch dangling by threads of bark, the white wood of the break still pale and moist. He's right. That's hours old, maybe less. My pulse kicks up a notch.

"Could be hikers," I say, but I don't believe it.

"Could be." Morrison moves up beside me, scanning the terrain ahead. "Let's assume it's not. Different route down?"

I consider the options, mapping the terrain in my head. "There's a steeper path to the east. More exposure, harder going, but it comes out near the ranger station instead of the main trailhead."

"Your call."

I look at him, this Guardian operative who tracked me through miles of wilderness and is now deferring to my judgment about our escape route. There's trust in that, and competence, and something else that makes my chest feel tight. When was the last time someone looked at me like I was capable instead of broken?

"East path," I decide. "If they're watching the main trail, we'll bypass them."

We cut through dense manzanita that tears at our clothes and skin, dropping into a ravine that requires careful footing.

Morrison stays close, moving with the kind of awareness that says he's done this before in worse places. Once I lose my footing on loose scree, his hand shoots out to steady me, fingers firm around my upper arm. The touch lasts barely a second, but I feel the warmth of it, the strength, and then it's gone.

The ravine narrows ahead, water-smoothed rock slick with moisture. I test the first foothold, but my boot slips. Before I can catch myself, Flint's there—hands on my waist, steadying me, his chest against my back.

"Easy," he murmurs, voice low near my ear. "Let me help."

His hands don't leave as I find purchase, fingers splayed across my hips, thumbs pressing just above my belt. The touch is professional—practical—but heat blooms where he's holding me anyway, spreading through my body in a way that has nothing to do with exertion.

I make it across, but when I turn back, his eyes are dark with something that isn't tactical awareness.

Our hands meet as he crosses—his reaching, mine extended to help—and our fingers thread together naturally, palm to palm, calluses matching.

The contact holds longer than necessary. Long enough that I feel his pulse against mine, strong and steady. Long enough that the air between us thickens with awareness we're both pretending not to feel.

"Thanks," I manage.

"Anytime." His thumb brushes across my knuckles once before he releases me. "That's what Guardians do."

The words sound like a promise, and something in my chest loosens fractionally. Maybe I'm not alone in this after all. Maybe walking back into my nightmare doesn't mean walking back into it by myself.

We push on, and the mountain slowly releases us toward the world below, where explosive devices tick down to detonation and Marcus Greer waits to see if I'm brave enough or stupid enough to try stopping them.

I don't know which I am. But I'm about to find out.

FIVE

FLINT

____

The manzanita tears at my clothes as we push through the dense scrub, branches scratching across my face and arms with enough force to draw blood. Carolina moves ahead of me with the confidence of someone who knows this terrain intimately, picking paths that barely exist, reading the landscape in ways that take years to learn.

I keep my focus split between following her and watching our six, hand never far from my Glock, every sense tuned to the possibility of contact.

The fresh break we spotted twenty minutes ago wasn't an accident. Someone came through here recently, moving fast enough to be careless about leaving a sign of their passage behind.

They're either inexperienced or they don't care about being tracked. Neither option is good. Inexperienced means unpredictable, and not caring means confident they won't be caught—or that catching them won't matter because they'll have accomplished their mission first.

We drop into a steep ravine where water has carved a channel through limestone and granite, the walls rising fifteen feet on either side. Carolina navigates it with the ease of a mountain goat, boots finding purchase on wet rock that looks impossible to climb.

I follow more carefully, testing each hold before committing my weight. The pack on my shoulders shifts as I move, and the paracord bracelet catches on a jutting rock, yanking hard enough to dig into my wrist. I free it without stopping, the familiar bite of pain centering me the way it always does.

Promises I didn't keep. People I failed to save. The bracelet reminds me every day that hesitation kills, that being too late is the same as being wrong, and that I can't afford either one.

Carolina reaches the top of the ravine and extends a hand down to help me up the last few feet. I take it, her grip strong and calloused, and for a moment we're close enough that I can smell the sweat and pine sap on her skin, see the flecks of gold in her hazel eyes. Then she's moving again, releasing my hand and turning to scan the terrain ahead.

"Ranger station is another hour at this pace," she says quietly. "Trail opens up in about ten minutes—we'll be more exposed, but we can move faster."

I check my watch. We've been moving for fifty minutes since breaking her camp, which puts us at roughly eleven hours until Device Three's estimated detonation. Assuming the estimate is accurate, which it might not be. Greer could have lied about the timing just to add pressure, or the device could be on a variable timer that adapts based on environmental factors.

Carolina would know, but I'm not going to ask her right now when I need her focused on survival.

"How exposed?" I ask.

"Open slope, scattered oak and pine. Good sight lines in both directions." She meets my eyes. "If someone's watching for us, they'll see us coming."

"Can we avoid it?"

"Not without adding another hour." She pauses. "Your call."

I run the tactical calculation quickly. Another hour means more time for whoever left that broken branch to position themselves or to find Carolina's vehicle and set up an ambush at the extraction point.

"We move fast through the open ground," I decide. "Spread out, staggered positions, use what cover there is. If we take fire, you get to ground, and I'll suppress. Don't try to be a hero—that's my job."

Her jaw tightens. "I can handle myself."

"I know you can. But I'm better equipped and trained for direct action, and Guardian HRS pays me to take bullets so people like you can do the jobs only you can do." I soften my tone slightly. "I need you alive and functional at that device. That means I take the risks out here."

She looks like she wants to argue, but pragmatism wins. "Fine. But if you get killed being noble, I'm going to be really annoyed."

"Noted." I gesture ahead. "Lead on."

We emerge from the ravine into rolling terrain covered in dry grass and scattered trees. The sun is climbing toward midday, heat building despite the elevation, and the vegetation has that parched quality that comes with California's endless summers.

Every footfall on the dry grass sounds too loud, and the openness makes the back of my neck itch with awareness. This is bad ground for what we're doing—too much exposure, too many angles for an ambush, nowhere to hide if things go sideways.

Carolina moves to the right flank, putting twenty yards between us, and we advance in a leapfrog pattern. She moves forward while I cover, then I advance while she watches.

It's slower than running straight through, but it gives us overlapping fields of fire and makes us harder to pin down. She adapts to the pattern immediately —no instruction needed —and I file that away as more evidence of her competence. Army training, even years removed, leaves its mark.

We're halfway across the open slope when I catch movement in my peripheral vision. Left side, maybe a hundred yards upslope, something that doesn't match the pattern of swaying grass and shifting branches. I freeze and signal Carolina to stop and get down. She drops immediately behind a fallen oak, Sig appearing in her hand like magic.

I scan the area carefully, looking for whatever triggered my instinct. There—behind a cluster of manzanita, a shape that's too solid, too regular. Human form, staying low, trying for concealment but not quite achieving it. I glass the position with my binoculars, bringing the figure into focus.

Man, mid-thirties, tactical clothing, rifle with scope. He's watching the trail below and hasn't seen us yet because we took the alternate route. But he's positioned exactly where he needs to be to ambush someone coming down from Carolina's camp on the main trail.

My radio crackles softly on my hip. "Flint, this is Base. Status?"

I key the radio, keeping my voice barely above a whisper. "Contact. Single hostile, armed, appears to be in a surveillance position on the main trail approach. We've bypassed his position, but he's between us and extraction."

"Copy. Helicopter is fifteen minutes out. Can you avoid engagement?"

I study the terrain, calculating angles and distances. We're downslope from the hostile, and if we continue on our current route, we'll pass within fifty yards of his position. That's well within rifle range, and if he's even marginally competent, he'll spot us.

"Negative. We either engage or find another route that adds significant time."

Carolina has moved up beside me in a low crouch. She leans in, her shoulder against mine, and whispers directly in my ear. "There's a draw thirty yards ahead that cuts down toward the ranger station. Steep, but it gives us cover and gets us below his sight line."

Her breath is warm against my ear, and I'm aware of her proximity in ways I shouldn't be during a tactical situation. I force my focus back to the terrain and spot the draw she's referencing—a deep cut in the hillside where runoff has carved a channel. It'll be rough going, but she's right—it offers concealment.

"We're taking an alternate route," I key my comm, reporting in. "Should reach extraction in twenty minutes." I meet Caro's eyes. "You lead. Fast and quiet. If he spots us and opens fire, you keep moving and don't look back."

"Flint—"

"That's an order." The words come out harder than I intended. "You're the mission. Everything else is secondary."

She holds my gaze for a long moment, something complicated moving behind her eyes, then nods once. We move toward the draw in a fast crouch, using every scrap of cover the terrain offers. The grass is dry enough to crackle under our boots, and I'm acutely aware that sound carries in this open country.

Every step feels like shouting our position.

We're ten yards from the draw when the air splits apart with a rifle's crack. The round snaps past my head, close enough to shear the breath from my lungs. Instinct takes over. I slam into Carolina, driving her toward the ravine, my body covering hers as dirt and rock explode around us.

We tumble down the embankment, gravity and momentum taking control. Her pack slams into my ribs, a jolt that drives the air from my lungs. My elbow hits rock—pain flares white-hot up my arm. More shots crack overhead as we slide, stones skittering past in a gritty roar.

We hit the bottom hard, tangled in each other and the mess of gear.

For a heartbeat, everything stops—the gunfire, the tumble, even thought.

She's beneath me, her breath hot against my throat, heartbeat hammering against my chest where we're pressed together. The scent of her—salt, sweat, fear, life—hits me like a punch, overwhelming in its intensity.

One of my thighs is wedged between hers, my hand somehow ended up cradling the back of her head, protecting it from the rocks, and the other is splayed across her ribs, feeling every rapid breath she takes.

Her eyes are wide, hazel gone dark with adrenaline and something else—something that mirrors the heat spiking through my own body.

For a fraction of a second, neither of us moves. We're frozen in this moment, hyperaware of every point of contact: my chest against hers, her legs tangled with mine, the way her hands have fisted in my vest, like she's holding on or pulling me closer —I can't tell which.

Heat blooms fast and low, primal and immediate—pure biology responding to survival, to proximity, to the feel of her body under mine.

Wrong time, wrong place, but my body doesn't care about tactical situations. It only knows she's soft where I'm hard, alive and warm and right there.

Her lips part, whether to speak or just to breathe, I don't know, and I realize with sudden, unwanted clarity that I want to kiss her. Want it with an intensity that's completely inappropriate given that we're currently being shot at.

Focus, dammit. Focus.

The scent of dust and sweat fills my head, sharp and human and alive. Then training kicks back in. I roll off, my weapon coming up, the world narrowing again to angles, shadows, threat.

"You hit?" I snap, already scanning the rim of the draw for threats.

"No. You?"

"Negative." I key my radio. "Taking fire, one hostile with a rifle, we're in cover but pinned."

More rounds crack overhead, stitching across the rim of the draw, but the shooter doesn't have an angle on us yet. He's firing blind, trying to keep us suppressed while he repositions. I estimate his location based on the sound—still roughly where I first spotted him, which means he hasn't moved to flank us yet. That gives us maybe thirty seconds before this position becomes untenable.

"There's another one," Carolina says, and I follow her gaze to see a second figure moving fast down the slope from a different angle. They're trying to box us in — classic hammer-and-anvil — and they've got the angles to make it count. If they coordinate even moderately well, we're in serious trouble.

I decide in a fraction of a second. "Move. Down the draw, fast as you can. I'll slow them down."

"Like hell—"

"Carolina." I grab her arm, forcing her to look at me. "You die here, those devices go off, and more people die. You're the only one who can stop them. You run to the clearing below—the one with the lone aspen and the flat—get there and stay low. I'm going to make sure you get the chance to do what you do best."

Her jaw tightens. Fear flickers, then something like stubborn resolve settles over her face. "Don't you dare die on me, Morrison."

"Not planning on it." I release her arm and shift position to get a better angle on the approaching shooters. "Now move."

I activate my mike and report in, calm and clipped. "Command, this is Flint. We're taking hostile contact, two shooters—moving to box. Sending subject to a clearing at the lower draw for immediate extraction. Request QRF and medic to grid point Delta-three, ETA two minutes. I'm engaging to delay."

Static answers, then the terse acknowledgment I need. "Copy, Flint. QRF en route."

I shove Carolina toward the path. She moves like a machine, boots finding purchase in loose dirt, pack thumping against her back. I angle myself between her and the shooters, weapon up, eyes slicing the slope for movement.

The sound draws fire from the first shooter, rounds kicking up dirt twenty yards from her position. I return fire, three controlled pairs at the muzzle flash, and have the satisfaction of seeing the shooter duck back into cover.

The second shooter is closer now, maybe forty yards and closing fast. I shift aim and engage, forcing him to dive behind a boulder. My magazine runs dry, and I drop it, slamming a fresh one home without taking my eyes off the threats.

The drill is so ingrained it's automatic—muscle memory built through thousands of repetitions until it's faster than thought.

Carolina is ten yards, and then five, from the clearing. She hits it and drops into the scrub, flattening herself the way we train—small, controlled, ready for pickup.

"Flint, we have visual on your position," the radio crackles. *"Helicopter inbound, sixty seconds."*

I key the mic while tracking the second shooter. "Subject is in place. I'm holding position to cover her movement."

"Negative. Break contact and extract."

"Not leaving her exposed." I fire again as the first shooter tries to advance. The round catches him somewhere center mass—he staggers—but he's wearing body armor and stays on his feet. Damn it. "Get the subject out. I'll be right behind her."

That's a lie. If these two are competent, they'll keep me pinned here while Carolina extracts, and that's fine.

My job is to get her out, not to make it home myself.

The bracelet on my wrist digs into my skin as I brace my shooting position, and I think about the promises I didn't keep three years ago, the people I was too slow to save.

Not this time. Not her.

SIX

FLINT

Movement to my left—the second shooter is trying to use the terrain to flank me. I pivot and engage, two rounds that force him back, but it exposes me to the first shooter.

A round catches my vest high on the right side, just below my shoulder. The ceramic plate catches most of it, but the kinetic energy is enough to spin me partway around and drive the breath from my lungs. The impact feels like getting hit with a sledgehammer, pain radiating through my chest and shoulder.

I stay on my feet through sheer stubbornness, returning fire even as my right arm goes partially numb from the impact. The second shooter is moving again, trying to close the distance while I'm hurt.

I track him, squeeze the trigger, and see him go down hard. Not dead—he's moving, trying to crawl to cover—but out of the fight for now.

The first shooter opens up on full auto, hosing my position with rounds that kick up dirt and shred vegetation. I flatten myself against the side of the draw, making myself as small a target as possible, and wait for a reload.

The instant the firing stops, I'm up and moving, running in a low crouch down the draw after Carolina. Pain radiates from my shoulder with every jarring step, but I've been hurt worse and kept moving.

Evac is closing in. The distinctive thump of rotors echoes off the hillsides. It comes in fast and low, heading for the clearing.

More shots from behind me, but they're poorly aimed, desperation fire from a shooter who's lost his tactical advantage. I don't return fire, just keep moving, eating up ground with long strides that send jolts of pain through my bruised ribs and shoulder.

The draw opens up ahead, spilling into flatter ground. The helicopter is touching down.

Carolina is there, fifty yards ahead, running flat out for the aircraft. Her pack bounces on her shoulders, and her braid has come partially loose, dark hair whipping in the rotor wash. She's twenty yards from the helicopter when I see the third shooter.

He comes out of the tree line to her left, rifle shouldered, tracking her movement. Time compresses and expands simultaneously, the way it does in combat when adrenaline kicks perception into overdrive.

He acquires his target. Finger tightens on the trigger. Carolina runs with no idea he's there.

I'm moving before conscious thought kicks in, angling to intercept, weapon coming up, even though I'm too far for an accurate shot at a running sprint. I fire anyway, three rounds that go wide but close enough to make him flinch. His rifle swings toward me, tracking the new threat, and in that split second, his attention is off Carolina.

His muzzle flash is bright even in daylight. I feel the impact in my vest again—two rounds center mass that knock me off my feet. The ceramic plates hold, but the force is like getting hit by a truck. I hit the ground hard, air driven from my lungs, vision graying at the edges from the impact.

But I keep firing even as I fall, and my rounds find him this time —I see the impacts stitching across his chest, see him drop.

Suddenly, hands are on me, pulling at my vest. I try to push them away before I realize it's Carolina. She's on her knees beside me, face pale, eyes wide with fear that's for me, not herself. Her hands check for wounds, finding the dented plates in my vest.

"Stay with me." Her words tumble out fast and urgent. "Goddammit. You don't get to do this. You don't get to save me and then die on me. That's not how this works."

"M'okay," I manage, though my chest feels like it's been caved in. "You need to... get to the helicopter."

"Fuck the helicopter." Her voice breaks on the words. "I'm not leaving you."

Guardian HRS personnel are suddenly there, two operators I recognize. One of them—Jenkins—kneels on my other side, combat medic kit already open. The other provides security, weapon up and scanning for threats.

Strong hands pull Carolina back gently but firmly, but she fights them for a second before training or sense kicks in. She lets them work, but stays by my side.

Jenkins cuts away my vest, exposing the massive bruising already forming across my chest and shoulder. His face stays professionally neutral, but I see his jaw tighten fractionally. "Two impacts, plates held. Significant blunt trauma to the thoracic cavity. Possible rib fractures."

He works quickly, checking for internal bleeding, assessing breathing. The pain is intense—every breath feels like knives in my chest—but nothing feels catastrophically wrong. Broken ribs maybe, bruised organs definitely, but I'm not dying.

"We need to move him now," Jenkins says.

They lift me in a practiced carry. The world tilts sickeningly. Carolina is there beside me, her hand still gripping mine, her face the only thing I can focus on through the pain and gathering darkness. She says something, but the helicopter noise is too loud and my hearing seems muffled, like I'm underwater.

We reach the aircraft. Hands pull me inside, laying me on the deck. Jenkins works on me, setting up an IV, monitoring vitals. Carolina climbs in and refuses to be moved from beside me, her hand back in mine, her face close enough that I can see the tears she's fighting.

"You saved my life," she says, and I can read her lips even though I can barely hear her over the rotors. "You took bullets for me."

"That's what Guardians do," I try to say, not sure if the words make it out of my mouth.

Her other hand comes up to cup my face, thumb brushing across my cheekbone, and the touch is gentle in a way that makes my chest ache beyond the physical pain. "You're not allowed to die, you hear me? We have a deal."

I want to tell her that I'll be fine, that I've been through worse, that chest impacts aren't going to keep me down. But the pain medication Jenkins pushed is hitting hard, gray turning to black at the edges of my vision, and it's taking all my energy just to stay conscious.

Her face is the last thing I see before everything fades—hazel eyes fierce with determination and fear, jaw set in that stubborn line I'm already learning to recognize, beautiful and strong and alive because I got to her in time.

I check my watch through the blood and adrenaline haze. 8:15 PM. We've been moving for over four hours since leaving Carolina's camp. The mission clock is ticking—nineteen hours until Device 3, maybe less.

The thought follows me down into darkness.

I surface to fluorescent lights and an antiseptic smell, the distinctive atmosphere of medical facilities everywhere. My chest is screaming at me, a deep throbbing ache that radiates from sternum to spine, and my right shoulder feels like it's been through a meat grinder. I try to sit, but a hand presses firmly against my sternum, keeping me flat.

"Easy." CJ's voice is calm and authoritative. "You've got three cracked ribs and extensive soft tissue damage. You're not going anywhere fast."

I force my eyes to focus on him. He's standing beside the bed in what looks like Guardian HRS's medical facility, arms crossed, expression caught between concern and annoyance. Behind him, there's monitoring equipment, IV stands, the clean efficiency of a well-equipped trauma bay.

"Carolina?" My voice comes out rough, throat dry as sand.

"She's fine. No injuries beyond some scrapes and bruises." CJ's expression softens fractionally. "She's being briefed by the FBI now. You got her out clean, Flint. The mission is still viable."

I try to process that through the fog of pain and whatever drugs they've given me. "Timeline?"

"Ten hours until Device Three's estimated detonation. Sutton identified the location—Camp Cielo Azul, wilderness education center in the Los Padres foothills. FBI is evacuating the area now." He pauses. "She wants to see you before they transport her to the site."

"The hostiles?"

"Two dead, one critical. They were Greer's people. Former military, dishonorable discharges, history of anti-government extremism. Greer has more resources than the FBI initially thought." CJ's jaw tightens. "You stopped an assassination."

I process that, thinking about the moment when the third shooter had Carolina in his sights. Another second and she'd be dead. Another second, and the only person who can stop Greer's devices would be gone. The bracelet on my wrist—somehow still there despite everything—feels heavier.

"I need to be there," I say, trying to sit up again. "At the device site. She'll need protection."

"You can barely breathe without wincing. You have multiple rib fractures and—"

"I can stand. I can shoot. That's all I need." I override his objection with the flat certainty of someone who's made the decision and won't be swayed. "She goes into that situation, and I go with her. Non-negotiable."

CJ studies me for a long moment, and I can see him reading things in my face I didn't mean to show. "You're compromised," he says finally.

I don't deny it. Can't deny it, not after taking multiple rounds to keep her alive, not after seeing her face in those last seconds before I blacked out. "I'll die before I let something happen to her."

"Doc Summers has to clear you. You've got two hours before transport. Hope you heal fast." CJ sighs, recognizing a lost argument when he sees one. "The medic will fit you with a compression wrap for your ribs, load you up with enough painkillers to function. But if you can't perform—if Doc Summers doesn't clear you—I'm pulling you. Understood?"

"Understood."

He heads for the door, then pauses. "Caro stayed with you the whole flight back. Wouldn't let go of your hand. Fought the medics when they tried to move her aside." His expression is unreadable. "Thought you should know."

Then he's gone, and I'm alone with the pain and the drugs and the memory of Carolina's hand in mine, her voice fierce and desperate: *You don't get to die on me.*

I close my eyes and focus on breathing through the pain, building a wall between the agony in my chest and the clarity I'll need to function.

I've operated through worse—a compound fracture in Mosul, shrapnel in my back in Kandahar, and three broken ribs in Syria.

Pain is just information, and information can be managed, compartmentalized, and filed away until the mission's done.

The door opens again. I expect a medic. Instead it's Carolina.

She's cleaned up since the extraction—fresh clothes that someone must have provided, her hair braided neatly again, the blood and dirt washed away. But her eyes are red-rimmed, and she moves to my bedside with an urgency that says she ran here the moment they let her.

"Hey," I say, inadequate but all I've got.

"You're an idiot." Her voice shakes. "A noble, stupid, heroic idiot."

"Probably."

She pulls a chair close to the bed and sits heavily, like her legs won't hold her anymore. For a long moment, she looks at me, processing everything—the ambush, the impacts to my vest, how close it came to going completely sideways. Then her hand reaches out and finds mine, fingers threading through mine, and the touch grounds something in me I didn't realize was floating.

"Thank you," she says quietly. "For what you did. For getting me out."

"That's what—"

"If you say 'that's what Guardians do' one more time, I'm going to hit you." But there's no heat in it, just exhaustion and relief and something else I can't quite name. "You took bullets for me. Multiple impacts that could have killed you. That's not just doing your job—that's... that's something else."

"You're worth it. The mission is worth it. I'd do it again." I turn my hand in hers so I can squeeze gently.

"I know." Her thumb brushes across my knuckles. "That's what scares me."

We sit in silence for a moment, her hand in mine, the weight of everything unspoken hanging between us. I'm aware of the clock ticking down, of the device waiting at Camp Cielo Azul, of the fact that in a few hours she'll be the one in danger while I try to keep her alive.

But right now, in this quiet moment, there's just this—her hand in mine, both of us breathing, both of us alive when we came too close to the alternative.

"I'm coming with you," I say finally. "To the device site. CJ tried to bench me, but I shut that down."

"Morrison, your ribs—"

"Will hold together long enough. I've operated through worse." I meet her eyes. "You're going to be vulnerable while you work on that device. Greer's people already tried to kill you once. I'm not letting you face the next attempt without me there."

She looks like she wants to argue, but something in my expression stops her. Instead, she leans forward, resting her forehead against our joined hands, and I feel her shoulders shake with a breath that might be a laugh or a sob.

"Okay," she whispers. "Okay. We do this together."

"Together," I agree, and ignore the way my chest tightens at the word—emotional, not physical.

Doc Summers arrives eventually, brisk and compact, brown hair twisted into a knot that looks as if it's been redone three times today already. She waves Carolina toward the door with that deceptively gentle tone that always means now, not later.

Carolina hesitates, but one sharp look from the Doc sends her out.

I'm propped against the table, shirt off, chest a masterpiece of purple and black bruising. Summers doesn't bother with preliminaries—she's already pulling gloves on.

"You Guardians," she mutters, probing my ribs with practiced efficiency that still makes me wince, "one of these days I'm putting a revolving door on the trauma bay. You think Kevlar makes you immortal."

"Just durable," I answer, trying for humor.

She snorts. "Durable doesn't mean bulletproof. You've got three cracked ribs and bruising that goes down to the bone." Her fingers find a particularly tender spot, and I can't suppress a grunt. "Multiple impacts like that could have caused cardiac contusion, pneumothorax, all sorts of fun complications. You're lucky."

"Nothing I haven't worked through before."

"Don't give me that Guardian stoicism." She starts wrapping my ribs with compression bandages, the support immediately helping with the pain. "You people act like pain's a personality trait."

I let her finish the wrapping, saying nothing. When she steps back, she folds her arms, measuring me. "Regulations say you're off active duty until those ribs heal."

"Regulations also give you discretion for field necessity," I remind her.

"Field necessity," she repeats, exasperation thick. "You mean you're short-staffed and too stubborn to sit down for three days."

I lift a brow. "You said it, not me."

For a long moment, she studies me, weighing risk against reality. Finally, she sighs, pulling off her gloves. "Fine. You're cleared for limited field ops. No hand-to-hand combat, no jumping out of helicopters, and if you puncture a lung being heroic, you crawl back here on it. Understood?"

"Yes, ma'am."

She shakes her head, but there's the faintest smile tugging at her mouth. "You Guardians never learn. Try not to die before I get a coffee break."

"Wouldn't dream of it."

She's halfway out the door when she calls back, "Tell Carolina she owes me a new roll of bandages. She was pacing a groove in the floor with worry."

I can't help the slight grin that follows. The compression wrap helps stabilize everything, and with the pain medication kicking in, I can move without feeling like my chest is caving in. Ugly, painful—but functional. Good enough for now.

Good enough.

CJ comes back with my gear—fresh clothes, a new vest since mine took too many rounds, weapons cleaned and reloaded. He watches me dress with the critical eye of someone assessing whether I'm fit for duty, but whatever he sees must satisfy him because he doesn't object.

"Transport leaves in twenty minutes," he says. "FBI has the site secured. Sutton will have full support—bomb techs standing by, medical on standby, Guardian HRS team for security. Your job is to keep her breathing while she works."

"That's the plan."

"Flint." He waits until I meet his eyes. "She's going to be focused on that device. Tunnel vision. She won't be watching for threats. That's on you, injured or not."

"I know."

"And if you go down, there's no one else who can protect her the way you will."

"Then I won't go down." I check my Glock, chamber a round, and holster it. "Anything else?"

He shakes his head slowly. "Don't come back in a body bag."

It's as close to sentiment as CJ ever gets, and I nod once in acknowledgment. Then I'm moving toward the transport area where Carolina and the rest of the team are waiting.

Carolina looks up when I enter the staging area. She doesn't say anything, just moves to my side like it's the most natural thing in the world. Like we're already a team, already partners in whatever comes next.

The helicopter is warming up outside, rotors beginning their familiar beat. Ten hours. Maybe less. And at the end of them, either Carolina disarms a device that's designed to kill her, or people die, and Greer wins.

Not acceptable.

I follow her out to the aircraft, my hand finding the small of her back briefly as she climbs aboard—a touch that's protective and possessive. She settles into a seat, and I take the one beside her, close enough that our shoulders brush.

Close enough that I can move to shield her if needed.

Close enough that I can feel her breathing and know she's alive.

The helicopter lifts off, and through the open door, Guardian HQ falls away beneath us, the California coast stretching endlessly to the west. We're heading inland, toward the mountains, toward the wilderness education center where children learn to tie knots, identify plants, and feel safe in nature.

Toward the place where Greer left a bomb with Carolina's name written all over it.

I check my weapons one more time, settling into the pre-mission headspace where everything narrows to the objective. Protect Carolina. Keep her alive. Let her do what only she can do.

The bracelet on my wrist catches the light, and I run my thumb over it once—a prayer or a promise or both.

Not too late this time.

Not her.

SEVEN

CAROLINA

The FBI field office in Lompoc is organized chaos, dozens of people moving through spaces designed for half that number. I sit in a conference room with laminate tables and fluorescent lights, a cup of terrible coffee cooling in front of me while Special Agent Monica Parker walks me through what they know.

She's mid-forties, sharp-eyed, and moves with the economy of someone who's spent twenty years in federal law enforcement. Her last name makes my chest tighten—same as Private Noah Parker, though she hasn't mentioned any relationship, and I'm not going to ask.

"Marcus Greer has been in our custody for thirty-six hours," Parker says, pulling up photos on the large screen at the front of the room.

Greer's face appears, older than I remember but still recognizable. The same cold eyes, the same arrogant set to his jaw.

"He was caught attempting to place Device One at the Lompoc Water Treatment Facility. Our techs were able to disarm it, but barely. The trigger system was unlike anything they'd encountered."

Because it's mine.

Because I designed it to be adaptive, to think, to counter standard EOD protocols.

I designed it to teach my students to think three steps ahead and never assume they knew everything about a device just because they'd seen one like it before. And now Greer has weaponized that teaching, turned it into something that kills the very people I tried to train to survive.

"Device Two detonated at the San Luis Obispo electrical substation," Parker continues. "One fatality—a security guard who was on patrol when it went off. The detonation was remotely triggered, which tells us Greer has a partner or partners still active."

The guard's photo appears on screen. Michael Reyes, forty-two, married, father of three. I force myself to look at his face, to not turn away from what my design helped accomplish.

He's dead because of me—not directly, but the connection is there, undeniable. My innovation, my cleverness, my need to create something that would save lives has been twisted into something that takes them.

"We've identified Greer's likely targets based on his interrogation and known connections," Parker says, and more photos appear— infrastructure sites, government buildings, places that would cause maximum disruption and casualties. "But he's talking in riddles, and we believe you're the key to decoding them."

She pulls up the transcripts I saw on Flint's tablet in the wilderness, and I read through them again with attention to detail I didn't have time for before.

Greer's words are carefully chosen, each phrase loaded with meaning that only someone who knows our shared history would catch. *"The Girl Scout always comes prepared"*—he called me that for three years, mocking my thoroughness while simultaneously resenting it. *"Where Girl Scouts earn their badges"*—Camp Cielo Azul, where I spent weekends teaching kids skills that might save their lives someday.

"He's pointing to the camp," I say, the certainty settling cold in my gut. "Device Three is at Camp Cielo Azul. It's a wilderness education center about forty miles east of here, in the Los Padres foothills."

Parker's expression sharpens. "You're sure?"

"He knew I volunteered there. Made jokes about it, said I was wasting my time teaching kids when I could be doing real work." The bitterness in my voice surprises me. "He's chosen locations that have personal meaning, places that force me to face what my design can do. A training facility where I taught. A substation that powers the base where I served. And now a place where kids learn to survive in the wilderness—using skills I taught them."

"He's targeting you specifically," Parker says, and it's not a question. "This is personal revenge disguised as domestic terrorism."

"Yes." I meet her eyes. "He wants me to come. Wants me to try to disarm his devices. Either I fail and prove I'm the fraud he always said I was, or I succeed, but more people die because Device Four is still out there. Either way, he wins."

Parker leans back in her chair, processing. "We've already begun evacuating Camp Cielo Azul. There were fifty-two people on site— staff and a youth group from Bakersfield. The evacuation should be complete within the hour."

"What about Device Four?" I ask. "Has he given any indication of where it is?"

"Nothing concrete. More riddles about *'where imports become exports'* and *'the Gateway to the Pacific.'* Our analysts think he's referencing a port facility, possibly San Diego or Long Beach. We're increasing security at both locations, but without more specific intel..." She trails off, the implication clear.

We're chasing shadows until we have something concrete.

The door opens, and Flint walks in, moving carefully, one hand pressed subtly against his ribs. He's dressed in fresh tactical gear, a compression wrap visible under his shirt, moving with the controlled breathing of someone managing significant pain. But his eyes are clear, alert, tracking every person in the room before settling on me.

The weight of his attention is palpable, protective in a way that should irritate me but instead loosens something in my chest.

He's here. He's alive. He took multiple rounds to the vest for me, and he's still standing, still ready to do it again if necessary.

"Morrison," Parker acknowledges him with a nod. "Guardian HRS confirmed you'll be providing personal security for Ms. Sutton at the device site."

"That's correct." Flint moves to stand beside my chair, and I resist the urge to reach for his hand the way I did in the medical bay.

Professional. We need to stay professional here, even though every instinct I have is screaming to touch him, to confirm he's real and whole and not bleeding out in a helicopter anymore.

Parker walks us through the tactical plan—Guardian HRS will establish a perimeter around the device location, FBI bomb techs will be on standby, but I'll be the primary. Medical evacuation is staged a mile out. It's thorough and professional and exactly what I'd expect from federal law enforcement, but underneath it all is the awareness that we're racing a clock we can't see and playing a game where Greer wrote all the rules.

"We transport in thirty minutes," Parker says, standing. "Ms. Sutton, you'll ride with our tactical team. Morrison, you'll have separate transport with Guardian HRS personnel."

"Negative," Flint says, voice flat and brooking no argument. "Where she goes, I go. Same vehicle."

Parker's eyes narrow slightly. "That's not standard protocol—"

"I don't care about standard protocol. Three hours ago, Greer's people tried to kill her in the wilderness. They failed because I was there. She doesn't move without me within arm's reach until this is over." He meets Parker's gaze without blinking. "Non-negotiable."

There's a tension in the room, a contest of wills between federal authority and the kind of certainty that comes from someone who's already bled for their position. Parker looks to me, perhaps expecting me to object to being guarded so closely.

"He stays with me," I say quietly. "He's earned that right."

Parker considers for a moment longer, then nods curtly. "Fine. But you follow FBI protocols on site. We're in command."

"Understood," Flint says, though something in his tone suggests he'll follow those protocols exactly as long as they don't conflict with keeping me alive.

The meeting breaks up, people dispersing to their assigned tasks, and suddenly it's just Flint and me in the conference room. He's standing close enough that I can see the tightness around his eyes, the way he's breathing shallowly to minimize the pain from his ribs, the controlled movements that say the vest impacts were worse than he's letting on.

"You should be resting," I tell him. "Those ribs need—"

"What they need is to hold together for another twelve hours." He cuts me off gently but firmly. "After that, they can do whatever they want. But right now, I need to be functional."

I stand, closing the space between us until my pulse stumbles. The air thickens, charged with something that feels alive. He's close enough now that I can feel the heat coming off him, the subtle scent of soap and leather under the sterile tang of the infirmary.

He's taller than I remember—six-two, maybe six-three. I'm five-six, and to meet his eyes I have to tilt my head back, a movement that makes me acutely aware of everything else: the breadth of his shoulders stretching the fabric of his shirt, the corded muscle along his forearm, the faint rasp of stubble shadowing his jaw.

For a heartbeat, I just look at him. The stillness between us hums, my pulse syncing to the slow, controlled rhythm of his breathing. There's power in the way he holds himself—contained, deliberate, the kind of strength that doesn't need to announce itself.

Heat curls low in my stomach, sharp and sudden. I take in the scar peeking from beneath his collar, the square line of his throat when he swallows, the flicker of something unreadable in his eyes. It's too much and not enough all at once, the space between us a single breath from breaking.

"You took bullets for me."

"Yes." No hesitation, just fact. A flicker of dry amusement tugs at his mouth. "Technically multiple impacts," he adds, the corner of his lip lifting. "You keep rounding down."

The humor is quiet, threaded through the gravel of his voice, but it softens the space between us and turns the moment intimate instead of heavy.

"You could have died."

"But I didn't."

His voice is low, steady, the kind of calm that belongs to men who've faced death often enough to stop fearing it. His hand rises halfway, stopping just short of my cheek. The distance between his fingers and my skin might as well be a live wire.

"You're alive," he says, eyes locked on mine. "The mission's still viable. That's what matters."

The words are professional; the tone isn't. There's a rasp beneath them, a restrained warmth that hits harder than the confession itself. My breath catches, and I don't know if it's from gratitude or something far more dangerous. The heat from his body brushes against me, close enough that I can feel the thrum of his pulse in the air between us.

For a heartbeat, neither of us moves. His hand lingers, the shadow of touch trembling on the edge of becoming real. The noise of the medical bay fades until there's only the sound of breath—his and mine—intertwined, unspoken. Then he drops his hand, the spell breaking, professionalism snapping back into place.

"Get some rest, Carolina," he murmurs.

No one else says it like that—each syllable precise, deliberate, as if the name itself belongs to him. Everyone else calls me Caro, quick and casual, but from his mouth it sounds different.

Intimate. Possessive.

The air holds the echo of it, and the room feels warmer for it.

"You matter," I say, and my voice comes out rougher than intended. "What happens to you matters, Flint. You're not just... you're not just a tool to complete the mission. You're a person, and you nearly died, and I—" I stop, not sure how to finish that sentence.

I what?

Care about him?

Feel something for this man I met less than twelve hours ago?

I'm terrified by how much his survival means to me.

His hand completes its journey, cupping my cheek, thumb brushing along my cheekbone. The touch is gentle, almost reverent, and I lean into it before I can think better of it. Heat flickers between us—real, undeniable.

"I know," he says quietly, eyes steady on mine. "I feel it too."

"We just met." The protest comes out softer than I intend, more breath than sound. I don't move away.

"Doesn't matter." His thumb traces one more slow arc over my skin, grounding and electric all at once. "Combat warps time. A day out there feels like a lifetime. I've seen who you are when it counts— your courage, your instincts, your strength. And then…" His voice drops, roughening. "I almost watched you die. That changes things."

I draw in a shaky breath, the air between us thick with everything we aren't saying. The spark we've both tried to ignore hums like a live wire, impossible to untangle from the adrenaline still in our veins.

I could argue.

I could point out that adrenaline, proximity, and trauma are creating a false sense of connection.

I could be rational.

I could build the same walls I've lived behind for years, keep everything neat and safe and distant.

But I'm tired of being safe. Tired of being alone with ghosts that never stop whispering. Whatever this pull is between us, it feels too real to dismiss, like recognizing someone I've known in another life.

"After this is over," I say, the words surprising me even as I speak them, "we figure out what this is. If it's real, or just adrenaline and proximity messing with our heads."

His eyes hold mine, steady and unreadable, but something warmer sparks underneath.

"Deal." His thumb moves once more along my cheek, the faintest touch.

I think that will be the end of this moment, but his hand doesn't drop away. Instead, his fingers slide into my hair, cradling my head, and his eyes search mine—asking permission, giving me space to refuse.

I don't.

I close the distance between us, rising on my toes to meet him. The kiss is soft at first, tentative, just a brush of lips that sends electricity racing down my spine. Then his other arm comes around my waist, pulling me closer, and the kiss deepens.

He tastes like copper and antiseptic and something uniquely him. The kiss is slow, thorough, like he's memorizing me. His mouth moves against mine with the same confidence he brings to everything else—sure, steady, devastating in its gentleness.

When we finally break apart, we're both breathing hard. His forehead rests against mine, his hand still tangled in my hair, thumb stroking the sensitive skin behind my ear.

"After this is over," he murmurs against my lips, "we're definitely figuring this out."

"Definitely," I agree, and kiss him again—briefer this time, but no less intense.

"But first," he says, voice low, practical again, "we get through this."

"Agreed, survive this first," I agree, though even as I say it, part of me is already wondering what surviving might mean for us.

EIGHT

CAROLINA

THE DRIVE TO CAMP CIELO AZUL TAKES NINETY MINUTES, THE convoy of FBI and Guardian HRS vehicles winding through hills that turn from coastal scrub to oak woodland to pine forest.

I ride in an FBI suburban, Flint beside me in the back seat, his presence solid and grounding. We don't talk much—both of us are in pre-mission headspace, running through scenarios and contingencies, preparing for what's coming.

But his hand finds mine between the seats, fingers threading through mine, and that simple contact says everything words can't.

The camp is a collection of rustic buildings scattered across a meadow—main lodge, several cabin clusters, a dining hall with a peaked roof, storage buildings, and a covered pavilion for outdoor education.

Under different circumstances, it's idyllic, the kind of place kids remember forever as summer magic and nature adventures. Now it's a ghost town, evacuated and silent, waiting for the device that will either be disarmed or tear it apart.

The FBI establishes a command post in the parking area, tactical vehicles and equipment staged with military precision.

Bomb techs in heavy suits stand by, medical personnel prepping their equipment, Guardian HRS operators establish the perimeter.

It's a massive response, dozens of people, and the weight of their presence reminds me that failure here doesn't just mean my death—it means I fail all of them, fail the people who trusted me to be good enough.

Parker briefs me on the device location. "Staff spotted it in the main lodge. Wires visible behind the industrial refrigerator, timer display showing 4:32. Our techs did a preliminary scan—confirmed it matches the signature from Device One."

"I'll need to see it," I say, already running through approaches in my head. "Full workspace, good lighting, someone who can hand me tools without me having to look away from the device."

"I'll do it," Flint says immediately. "I've cross-trained on basic EOD support. I can hand you tools, hold things steady, whatever you need."

I start to object—he should be staying back, staying safe with those cracked ribs—but the look in his eyes stops me. He's not offering because he's the best person for the job. He's offering because he's not letting me face this alone, and arguing will waste time we don't have.

"Okay," I agree. "But you stay behind me, out of the primary blast radius if this goes wrong."

"Not acceptable."

"Flint—"

"If it goes wrong, we both go together or neither of us goes at all." His voice is gentle but immovable. "I'm not surviving you, Carolina. So you better make sure you get this right."

The words should be morbid, but instead they're oddly comforting. We're in this together. All the way. Whatever happens.

I suit up in minimal EOD gear—the full bomb suit would be too restrictive, too slow, and with Greer's modifications, it probably wouldn't save me anyway if I'm wrong. Just a vest, gloves, and a headlamp.

Flint checks his weapons, moving carefully but well despite the compression wrap around his ribs, and then we're walking toward the main lodge together.

The building is timber and stone, designed to blend with the natural environment, with large windows letting in the golden evening light. Under different circumstances, I'd admire the architecture. Now I note the exits, the cover positions, and the structural points where an explosion would do the most damage.

We enter through the main doors, boots echoing on the hardwood floors. The interior is organized chaos frozen in time—tables set for the next meal that never happened, a whiteboard with the day's activities still listed, backpacks abandoned in cubbies when the evacuation order came. It feels like walking through a museum of life interrupted, and the wrongness of it makes my skin crawl.

The kitchen is industrial-sized, designed to feed a hundred people at a time. Stainless steel counters, commercial stoves and ovens, and against the back wall, the refrigerator that's been pulled away from the wall to reveal the device.

I see it, and my stomach drops.

It's beautiful in the way that all sophisticated devices are—elegant, purposeful, every component serving a function. The housing is custom-machined aluminum, with a timer display LED that remains bright in dim lighting, and wires color-coded in the system I developed specifically for training.

But there are additions. Greer has made modifications that twist my design into something lethal.

A pressure plate under the primary housing that wasn't in my original design. A trembler switch is wired to the secondary circuit. A third component I don't immediately recognize, connected to what appears to be a cell phone receiver.

Three separate trigger mechanisms, each capable of detonating independently. Disable one wrong, and the others fire. It's diabolically clever, with Greer's grubby fingerprints all over it—his understanding of my teaching methods used against me, his modifications specifically designed to kill someone using my own protocols.

"Talk to me," Flint says quietly from behind me. "What are we looking at?"

"A nightmare." I pull out my tablet and snap photos from multiple angles. "Three trigger systems. The primary is my design—an adaptive trigger that learns and counters disarmament attempts. The pressure plate means I can't move it. The trembler means I can't let my hands shake. And the cell phone receiver means Greer or his partner can detonate remotely if they realize I'm here."

"Can you disarm it?"

"I don't know." The honest answer, the one that makes my hands want to shake and my breathing want to speed up. "I designed the primary system to be difficult but not impossible. But with these modifications... Greer knows how I think. He's anticipated my approaches. This thing is built specifically to kill me if I try."

Flint moves beside me, careful not to disturb anything, his presence warm and solid despite the obvious pain in his breathing. "But you're going to try anyway."

"I don't have a choice. This detonates, the building comes down, possibly triggering a wildfire in the surrounding forest. And Device Four is still out there." I force myself to breathe slowly, to center the panic before it can take root. "So yes. I'm going to try."

"Then tell me what you need."

I pull out my tool kit, laying out wire cutters, circuit testers, magnification goggles, everything I might need. "First, I need to identify which trigger is primary—which one controls the main charge. Then I need to bypass or disable the secondary triggers without activating the primary. Finally, I need to disarm the primary without triggering the fail-safes Greer built in."

"And if you're wrong about any of those steps?"

"Then we die instantly and won't know we made a mistake." I meet his eyes, seeing my own fear reflected there but also his steady confidence. "You should leave. Go back to the command post. Let me do this alone."

"Not happening."

"Flint—"

"Carolina." He takes my hand and squeezes it gently, though I can see the movement causes him pain. "I'm staying. Let me anchor you. You'll work better with me close. So use me. And trust that whatever happens, we face it together."

I want to argue.

I want to save him from what might be the last few minutes of his life. But the truth is, he's right. His presence grounds me, reminds me I'm not alone in this, and gives me something to fight for beyond just not failing again.

"Okay," I whisper. "Stay behind me. If I tell you to run, you run."

"If you tell me to run, we both run." He squeezes my hand once more, then releases it. "Now show me what you need me to do."

I position him behind and to the left, where he can hand me tools without being directly in line with the device. Then I kneel in front of the bomb, my headlamp illuminating the components in harsh LED white, and let my training take over.

First, assess. I use the circuit tester to trace the power flow, identifying which components are active, which are redundant, which are the actual threats, and which are designed to confuse.

The pressure plate is exactly what it looks like—a contact switch that closes the circuit when the device is lifted or moved. Simple, effective, and I'll have to work around it.

The trembler is more sophisticated —a mercury switch that detects vibration or sudden movement. I'll need to keep my hands steady, my breathing controlled, and no sudden motions.

That one I can manage if I focus.

The cell phone receiver is the wild card. If Greer or his partner is monitoring, if they realize I'm here working on the device, they could trigger it remotely at any time. I can't disable that one first because it's integrated into the primary trigger—cutting it would probably detonate the whole assembly.

"I need to start with the pressure plate," I say, narrating for Flint's benefit and my own. "It's the most straightforward. I'm going to shunt the contacts so it thinks it's still under load even after I disable it."

"What do you need?"

"Wire cutters, then the bypass bridge—it's the small metal clip in the red pouch."

His hands appear in my peripheral vision, offering the tools. I take them, position the bypass carefully across the contact points, then use the cutters to sever the connection to the primary circuit.

The device doesn't explode, which is always a good sign.

"Pressure plate neutralized," I say, allowing myself one slow breath of relief. "Next is the trembler."

This one is more delicate.

The mercury switch is housed in a small glass vial, and I need to stabilize it before I can disconnect it. I use a small amount of thermoplastic putty, warming it in my hands until it's pliable, then carefully wrap it around the vial to hold it in place. Every movement is glacially slow, my hands as steady as I can make them despite the adrenaline singing through my veins.

Flint's breathing behind me is slow and controlled, a rhythm I can match to keep my own breathing calm. His presence is a constant reminder that I'm not alone, that someone is here witnessing this, that my life has value beyond just being the person who fixes my own mistakes.

The thermoplastic sets after two minutes, which feels like two hours. I test the vial's stability gently, feeling for any movement. It's solid, held in place well enough that I can work with it. I trace the wires from the trembler to the primary circuit, identifying the connection point, and prepare to cut.

"This is the tricky part," I murmur. "The trembler is wired in series with the primary trigger. If I cut it wrong, if there's a voltage spike or a moment of disconnection, the primary might interpret it as a trigger signal."

"Can you prevent that?"

"I'm going to use a shunt to maintain voltage while I cut, then remove the shunt after the trembler is disconnected." I'm talking myself through it as much as explaining to him. "It should work. It worked in training simulations."

"But Greer knows your training simulations."

"Yes." That's the fear that's been gnawing at me since I saw this device.

Greer knows how I teach, knows the protocols I drill into my students, knows the exact approaches I'd use to disarm this. Has he built in a counter for this, too?

Is there a trap I'm not seeing?

But I don't have a choice. The clock is ticking, and people are counting on me to get this right.

I position the voltage shunt, double-check the connections, and cut the wire to the trembler. The device remains stable, no sudden changes. I remove the shunt carefully, and the trembler is isolated, disconnected, and no longer a threat.

"Two down," I say, and my voice shakes slightly. "One to go."

The primary trigger is my design, and I know it intimately—which should be an advantage but might be a curse if Greer anticipated my approach. I study the circuitry, looking for the modifications he's made, the ways he's adapted my elegant training system into something lethal.

There. I see it.

He's added a fail-safe that wasn't in my original design—a backup timer that activates if someone tries to disable the primary trigger using my standard teaching method. If I cut the wires in the order I taught him, in the sequence that every EOD student learns from me, the backup timer will drop to zero immediately.

He's betting I'll follow my own protocols. Betting I can't overcome my training even knowing it's compromised. It's psychological warfare wrapped in electronics, and I feel a flash of pure rage at his arrogance.

"I need to go off-script," I say to Flint. "He's modified this to counter my standard approach. I need to think like him instead of like me."

"Can you do that?"

I close my eyes briefly, forcing myself to breathe past the rush of panic. I have to let go of Caro Sutton—the teacher, the careful planner, the woman who worships procedure.

None of that will save us now.

Think like Marcus Greer. Reckless. Brilliant. The man who never met a boundary he didn't want to cross.

What would he do?

My first instinct is the same as always: check the obvious sequence, the clean linear logic. I start tracing it in my head, fingers twitching in rhythm with the pattern I drilled into my students. It should make sense—but it doesn't. The numbers won't align, the timing feels wrong.

"Come on, Greer," I mutter under my breath, frustration tightening my chest. "What did you hide?"

I retrace again, slower this time. Stop. Start over.

My gaze skims the components, lingering on those that fit too perfectly. He wouldn't leave the fail-safe there. He'd bury it under arrogance, in plain sight, but wearing a smirk.

The realization hits in a rush that feels almost physical. Not the obvious path. Not the logical progression. He'd tuck it somewhere no one disciplined would ever look—inside the piece that looks decorative, redundant, a flourish meant to distract.

"There," I whisper, pulse spiking. "I see you."

I hold my hand out, palm up. "Wire cutters."

Flint hands them to me, and I position them on the wire that shouldn't matter —the one most EOD techs would leave for last. I squeeze the handles slowly, feeling the resistance of the wire, and cut.

The timer display flickers. My heart stops.

Then it stabilizes, and I see the backup circuit go dark on my scanner. The fail-safe is disabled.

"The bastard," I whisper, almost admiring despite myself. "He hid it in plain sight, betting I'd overthink it."

Now just the primary trigger remains, and this one I know cold.

It's my design, unchanged by Greer's modifications except for being wired to a larger charge. I work through the disarmament sequence I developed over years of testing and refinement, each cut precise, each connection verified before moving to the next.

Time seems to slow and stretch, the world narrowing to just my hands and the device and the steady breathing of the man behind me.

Final wire. Final cut.

The timer goes dark.

The device lies silent—dead, harmless.

For a moment, I can't move. Then the tremor starts in my hands, adrenaline bleeding out of my system until all that's left is the hollow thud of my pulse.

Flint's hands find my shoulders, firm and steady, the heat of them cutting through the cold shock settling in my skin. The contact shouldn't matter as much as it does, but the moment he touches me, everything inside me shifts. Relief, exhaustion, something fiercer—all tangled together.

He's too close, his breath warm against my temple, the roughness of his palms a counterpoint to the careful strength in his grip. It feels intimate, too intimate for two people who've known each other less than a day. But I can't bring myself to pull away.

For once, I don't want distance. I want to turn into him, to let the solidity of his body erase the tremor in mine, to be held instead of holding everything together alone.

It shouldn't matter, but it does. God, it does.

"You did it," he says, voice roughened by more than exhaustion. "Carolina, you did it."

The sound of my name in his mouth slides through me like a caress, low and unguarded—each syllable spoken as if he's tasting it, claiming it. It wraps around me, grounding and electric all at once, and before I can stop myself, I'm leaning into his touch, chasing the warmth in his voice.

"There's still Device Four." But the words come out weak, exhausted. I disarmed Greer's death trap. I beat him. I didn't fail this time.

The FBI pours into the building, bomb techs moving to secure the device, Parker checking on us with sharp, concerned eyes. Someone wraps a blanket around my shoulders even though I'm not cold, and someone else is trying to get me to drink water.

But all I can focus on is Flint—his hands still anchored on my shoulders, his eyes fierce with pride and something deeper that steals the air from my lungs.

Without thinking, I lay my hand over his, the rough heat of his skin meeting my trembling fingers. The contact sends a pulse through me—warm, grounding, unbearably human.

For a heartbeat, neither of us moves. The world narrows to that single point of touch, the thud of my pulse against his palm, the shared breath hanging between us.

Then he moves—swift, sure—spinning me toward him.

I go willingly.

His arms come around me, strong enough to hold the shaking out of me. The impact is soft but all-consuming, the scent of dust and sweat and gunpowder still clinging to him.

I press my forehead against his chest, feeling the steady drum of his heart—strong, certain, alive. For the first time in longer than I can remember, I stop pretending I don't need anyone. I let the weight of his arms around me carry what I can't.

I let myself be held.

He doesn't speak, doesn't move to pull away. He just stands there, solid and unyielding, the kind of strength that asks for nothing and offers everything.

His hand comes up slowly, resting between my shoulder blades—not guiding, not restraining, just there. Steady. Present.

For once, I yield, letting someone else be the strong one while I breathe, shaking, against him.

"We need to find Device Four," I murmur against the fabric of his vest, my voice muffled, uneven.

"We will." His tone is quiet, sure, threaded with something gentler than command. "But first, you breathe." His palm presses slightly closer, an anchor more than an order. "You let yourself feel this. You won."

The words aren't about victory; they're about survival. And the way he says them—the warmth in his voice, the deliberate calm—feels like an offering. A promise that, for this heartbeat, I don't have to hold myself up alone.

I won.

The words feel foreign, unfamiliar. I'm not used to winning, not used to having the story end with everyone alive. But here we are—me, Flint, all the FBI and Guardian HRS personnel outside. No casualties. No failure.

Parker appears beside us, tablet in hand. "Ms. Sutton, I need you to look at something."

I pull back from Flint reluctantly and take the tablet. It shows photos of the disarmed device, close-ups of specific components. One of them makes my breath catch—a small note card, tucked under the primary housing where I would only find it after disarming the device.

I recognize Greer's handwriting immediately. The message is short, meant only for me:

"Congratulations, Girl Scout. You passed the first test. Device Four is where all journeys end and begin. Where the water meets the world. You have until sunrise to find it. Don't be late—you know I hate poor time management. -MG"

"Son of a bitch," I breathe. "This was all a test. A way to prove I'm good enough for whatever he's really planning."

"What does he mean about where journeys end and begin?" Parker asks.

I'm already turning the phrase over in my mind, hunting for the reference only I would recognize. *Where water meets the world. Journeys ending and beginning.*

The others might think of geography—any coastline, any harbor—but for Greer and me, it was always about systems, thresholds, transitions. The fragile seams where movement becomes exchange.

And then it clicks, sharp and immediate.

"The Port of Los Angeles," I say.

Parker frowns. "Out of every port on the coast, why that one?"

"Because it's where we started—and where we ended."

Images crash through memory: the heat-haze shimmer of container yards, the metallic smell of salt and diesel, the night Greer and I stood overlooking the cranes during training, arguing about control theory and chaos management.

He called it the heart of the machine, where the world's pulse could be stopped with a single disruption.

"It's the only port he ever cared about," I continue, voice steadier now. "His first field exercise was staged there. His final simulation—the one that got him pulled from the program—was supposed to mimic a cyber-physical strike at the Los Angeles terminal complex. He told me once that if he ever wanted to prove the system's fragility, he'd start there."

Parker exhales, understanding dawning.

"He's not talking about just any port," I finish quietly. "He's talking about *our* port. The one we built models around, the one we argued over for months. For Marcus Greer, the Port of Los Angeles isn't a target—it's the thesis. The beginning and the end of everything he's trying to prove."

Parker is already on her radio, coordinating with FBI offices in Los Angeles, requesting satellite imagery and port security footage. But I'm looking at the timer display in the photo, doing the math in my head.

If Device Four is as sophisticated as Device Three, maybe more so, I'm going to need most of that time just to find it in the sprawling chaos of one of the world's busiest ports.

"We need to move now," I say, standing despite the exhaustion pulling at me. "The port is massive. If we don't narrow down the location before we get there, we'll never find it in time."

Flint is already moving, checking weapons, keying his radio to alert Guardian HRS. "Transport time to Los Angeles?"

"Ninety minutes by helicopter," Parker says, already walking toward the exit. "We'll coordinate with LAPD and Port Authority en route. Ms. Sutton, you're with me. Morrison, Guardian HRS can follow in separate—"

"Same vehicle," Flint and I say simultaneously, and there's no room for argument in either of our voices.

Parker doesn't bother fighting it this time. We move as a unit toward the waiting helicopter, the evening air cool on my face, stars beginning to emerge overhead. Somewhere to the south, Device

Four is counting down toward detonation, and Greer is waiting to see if I'm smart enough, fast enough, brave enough to stop it.

I climb into the helicopter with Flint right behind me, his hand finding mine as soon as we're seated, and I hold on tight. We're not done yet. The real test is still waiting.

But I'm not alone anymore.

NINE

FLINT

The helicopter cuts through the night at full speed, the lights of Los Angeles sprawling beneath us like a vast constellation of gold and white. From this altitude, the city looks peaceful, orderly, but I know the reality is chaos barely contained—eight million people going about their lives with no idea that somewhere in the port district, a device is counting down toward catastrophe.

Carolina sits beside me, tablet on her lap, scrolling through satellite imagery of the Port of Los Angeles while conferring over a headset with FBI analysts.

She's been at it for the entire ninety-minute flight, narrowing down possible locations based on Greer's cryptic message and her understanding of his psychology. Dark circles under her eyes speak to exhaustion that goes beyond just today—this is years of carrying guilt and trauma, now compounded by hours of adrenaline and fear.

I want to tell her to rest, to close her eyes for ten minutes, but I know she won't.

Can't.

Not while the clock is ticking and people's lives depend on her being sharp enough to outthink a man who's had three years to plan his revenge.

My chest is a constant throb of pain despite the cocktail of drugs the medics loaded me with. The compression wrap helps hold everything together, but I can feel the cracked ribs protesting every movement, every breath.

I've been through worse, but those injuries came with the luxury of time to heal afterward. This one I need to function through for at least another eight hours, maybe more.

The paracord bracelet on my wrist catches my attention as I adjust my weapons for the third time.

The weave is blood-stained now, dark patches from where I held Carolina's hand in the helicopter during her extraction from the wilderness, from where I pressed it against wounds in the field. Another layer of meaning added to a talisman already heavy with failure and regret. But this time, maybe the blood represents something different.

Not failure.

Not being too late.

But being exactly on time, exactly where I need to be to keep someone alive.

"I think I've got it," Carolina says suddenly, pulling up a specific section of satellite imagery and expanding it. "Terminal 206, near the bulk cargo storage area. Look at this—there's a maintenance schedule showing electrical work was done two days ago, but Port Authority has no record of authorizing it. Someone got access under false pretenses."

Agent Parker leans in to study the image, her expression sharpening. "That area handles chemical shipments and industrial machinery. A device there could trigger secondary explosions, possibly take out multiple terminals."

"And it fits Greer's profile," Carolina adds. "Maximum disruption, maximum casualties, and it forces me to work near volatile materials. If I make a mistake disarming it, the blast could trigger a chain reaction."

"Can you disarm it without triggering anything?" Parker asks.

Carolina's silence is answer enough.

She doesn't know.

Won't know until she's looking at the device, assessing the threats, making split-second decisions that could save or end hundreds of lives.

"We'll get it done," I say quietly, and her eyes find mine across the cramped helicopter cabin. I see fear there, exhaustion, doubt. But also determination.

She'll face this because she has to, because no one else can, because running from her failures hasn't worked, and maybe confronting them will.

The helicopter begins its descent toward a staging area the FBI has established near the port.

Below, the port sprawls in a maze of steel and light—warehouses crouched low against the water, cranes towering like skeletal giants frozen mid-stride. Sodium lamps cast the docks in a jaundiced glow, turning the massive container ships into floating silhouettes, their hulls groaning softly with the tide.

The night is alive with the hum of generators and the distant clang of metal on metal. The Port of Los Angeles handles millions of containers annually, a constant flow of goods moving between ship and shore, the economic lifeblood of the region. And somewhere in that steel maze, Greer has hidden his final device.

We touch down in a parking lot that's been converted into a command post—FBI vehicles, LAPD bomb squad, Port Authority security, Guardian HRS operators. CJ is there to meet us, his expression grim in the harsh LED work lights.

"Terminal 206 is evacuated," he tells me as soon as I'm off the helicopter. "Port authority shut down operations in a three-terminal radius, but we can't evacuate the entire port without causing panic and gridlock. If this goes wrong, collateral damage will be significant."

"It won't go wrong," I say it with more confidence than I feel, but confidence is part of the job. "Carolina knows what she's doing."

"She's been awake for over twenty hours and working under extreme stress," CJ counters, then looks pointedly at my chest where the compression wrap is visible. "And you're barely functional with those ribs."

I look over to where Carolina is being briefed by Parker and port security, studying a physical map of Terminal 206's layout. Even exhausted, even scared, she's focused and professional. This is what she was trained for, what she's spent years mastering. The fact that Greer corrupted her work doesn't change her fundamental competence.

His eyes drop to my chest, to the way I'm carefully bracing against the injury to my ribs.

"I'm standing. That's enough." I meet his gaze steadily. "She needs someone she trusts beside her while she works. That's me. End of discussion."

CJ studies me for a long moment, seeing what I've been trying not to examine too closely myself. This stopped being just a mission somewhere between tracking her through the wilderness and taking bullets to keep her alive.

"Don't get her killed trying to protect her," he says finally. "And don't get yourself killed because you're too stubborn to admit you're compromised."

"Noted." I move toward where Carolina is waiting, each step a measured exercise in pain management and will.

She looks up when I approach, and something in her expression softens fractionally.

"Terminal 206 handles bulk cargo—industrial chemicals, machinery, raw materials. The maintenance records show electrical work near the chemical storage area, which is exactly where I'd place a device if I wanted maximum collateral damage." She traces a path on the map. "We go in on foot, Guardian HRS establishes perimeter, FBI bomb squad stays back unless I need them. It's going to be you and me, same as Camp Cielo Azul."

"Timeline?"

"Sunrise is at 6:52 AM, less than two hours from now. We need to move. Greer's note said '*don't be late,*' which could mean anything.

The device might be on a fixed timer, or it might have a variable trigger based on conditions we don't know yet."

"So we assume worst case and work fast."

"Yeah." She looks past me to the sprawl of terminals beyond the staging area.

TEN

FLINT

—the desire to protect me clashing with the need for someone she trusts beside her, fear of being responsible for another death tangled with the hard truth that she can't do this alone.

Finally, she nods once, accepting the terms I've laid out.

"Okay. Together."

"Together."

We gear up in silence, both of us falling into the rhythms of pre-mission preparation. I check my Glock, load fresh magazines, and ensure my radio is functioning.

Carolina assembles her tools, double-checking that everything she might need is accessible and organized. Around us, Guardian HRS operators and FBI agents move with purpose, everyone aware that the next few hours will determine whether this ends in success or catastrophe.

The drive to Terminal 206 takes fifteen minutes through deserted port roads, our convoy moving in darkness, sirens off. No point in advertising our presence to anyone who might be watching.

The terminal looms ahead, a massive warehouse structure surrounded by shipping containers stacked like building blocks, cranes frozen in position above. Floodlights cast harsh shadows, and the smell of diesel fuel and ocean salt is thick in the air.

Carolina sits beside me in the FBI suburban, close enough that our thighs press together with every turn. She's been quiet for most of the drive, reviewing device schematics on her tablet, but I've felt her awareness of me the whole time—the way her eyes track to me when she thinks I'm not looking, the way her hand keeps drifting toward mine before she pulls it back.

"Flint." Her voice is quiet, meant only for me despite the other occupants in the vehicle. "If something goes wrong in there—"

"Nothing's going wrong." I shift so I can look at her directly, our faces close in the dim interior. "You're going to disarm it, I'm going to keep you safe, and then we're both going home."

"You can't promise that."

"Watch me." I take her hand, threading our fingers together, and bring our joined hands to rest on my thigh. The contact grounds us both. "We've survived everything Greer threw at us so far. We're not stopping now."

She squeezes my hand hard enough to hurt, and I squeeze back. Her eyes are luminous in the darkness, reflecting the passing streetlights, and I can see fear there—but also determination. Trust. Something that looks like the beginning of love, though it's too soon for either of us to say it.

The vehicle slows as it approaches the terminal, and I have to release her hand. But the warmth of her fingers lingers on mine, and when we exit the vehicle, she stays close—close enough that I can feel her presence, close enough that I could reach for her in a heartbeat if needed.

Guardian HRS establishes a perimeter, operators fanning out to cover approaches and create a secure zone. FBI and port security set up a secondary perimeter farther out. If this goes wrong, they'll need to contain the blast and prevent secondary casualties. If it goes very wrong, nothing they do will matter—the chain reaction will devastate this part of the port.

Carolina and I approach the terminal building together, my hand never far from my weapon, her tool kit slung across her shoulders. The main entrance is secured with heavy locks, but port security has provided access.

We step inside a cavernous space filled with pallets of industrial materials, forklifts frozen in place, and the particular stillness that comes when a busy place suddenly goes silent.

"The electrical maintenance was logged for the northwest corner," Carolina says, consulting her tablet. "Near the chemical storage cages."

We move deeper into the terminal, our footsteps echoing on concrete floors, headlamps cutting beams through the darkness beyond the emergency lighting.

My instincts are on high alert, scanning for threats that might not be just electronic. Greer's people tried to kill Carolina. There's no reason to think he's abandoned that approach now.

The northwest corner houses a series of chain-link cages containing drums of industrial chemicals—acids, solvents, oxidizers, the kinds of materials that are individually inert, but catastrophic if mixed. A device here wouldn't just explode—it could trigger a toxic cloud, a firestorm, a chemical disaster that would make the blast radius secondary to the contamination zone.

And there, behind the cages, visible through the mesh, is the device.

It's larger than the one at Camp Cielo Azul, more sophisticated, clearly designed to be Greer's masterpiece. The housing is custom-machined steel, and the timer display LED is bright, showing 6:53.

But it's the additional components that make my stomach drop —what looks like shaped charges positioned to rupture specific chemical drums, a ventilation override that would spread toxic gases through the terminal's duct system, and what might be a radio-frequency trigger that could detonate the device remotely.

"Jesus," Carolina breathes, taking in the complexity. "He's trying to create a disaster that will be remembered for decades."

"Can you stop it?"

She's silent for a long moment, studying the device from multiple angles. "I think so. But it's going to take time, and I'll need absolute focus. Any distraction, any sudden threat, and I might make a mistake."

"Then I'll make sure there are no distractions." I key my radio, ignoring how the movement pulls at my damaged ribs. "I need complete security on this position. Nobody gets within fifty yards of this terminal. If anyone approaches who isn't an FBI agent or Port Authority employee with confirmed credentials, stop them. Use of force authorized."

Acknowledgments come back from the perimeter team. I turn to Carolina, seeing the fear and determination warring in her expression. "I'll be right here. Watching your back. Keeping you safe. You worry about the device."

She nods, setting down her tool kit and pulling out the equipment she'll need. I take up a position behind and to her left, weapon in hand, where I can see the approaches but won't interfere with her work. The position also keeps me out of the primary blast radius if things go wrong, though at this range, wrong means both of us die regardless of where I'm standing.

Carolina kneels in front of the device, her headlamp illuminating the components in harsh white light. She's silent for several minutes, just studying, assessing, building a mental map of how Greer constructed this and what approach she'll need to take.

I watch her work, seeing the competence and intelligence that first drew my attention in her file photo, seeing the courage it takes to face something specifically designed to kill her.

"Okay," she says finally, her voice steady. "Primary trigger is similar to Device Three but more sophisticated. He's added multiple fail-safes, redundant circuits, and what looks like a dead-man switch. I disable one component wrong and everything else fires simultaneously."

"What's your approach?"

"Systematic. Start with the components I'm most certain about, work toward the ones he's hidden or disguised. And pray I'm reading his psychology correctly, because this whole thing is designed to punish mistakes."

She reaches for her first tool, and her hand shakes slightly before she steadies it with visible effort. The tremor isn't exactly fear—it's exhaustion, an adrenaline crash, the accumulated stress of the last twenty-four hours. But she locks it down, forcing steadiness through sheer will, and begins.

The work is painstaking, each cut and disconnection requiring absolute precision. She narrates some of it for my benefit, though mostly she's talking herself through the steps, maintaining focus through verbalization. I listen with half my attention, the other half scanning our surroundings for threats. The terminal is quiet except for her voice and the distant hum of ventilation systems, but quiet doesn't mean safe.

Thirty minutes pass. Then an hour.

Carolina has disabled the secondary triggers she believes are causing the problem, bypassed several fail-safes, and isolated the primary timer mechanism.

Sweat beads on her forehead despite the cool air, and her hands are steady through pure concentration. She's working without the pressure plate and trembler complications from Device Three, but Greer has compensated by deliberately making the circuit path confusing, with redundant connections that could be vital or decoys.

My radio crackles softly. "Flint, we have a vehicle approaching from the south access road. Single occupant, not responding to hails."

I key the mic, keeping my voice low to avoid distracting Carolina. "Stop them at the perimeter. If they attempt to breach, disable the vehicle."

"Copy."

But something about it feels wrong. A single vehicle, not responding to challenges, is heading directly toward us?

It could be a lost civilian, could be port security who didn't get the message, or could be exactly what I'm afraid it is—Greer's partner making one last attempt to complete the mission.

"Carolina," I say quietly. "We might have company."

"How long can you keep them away?" Her voice is tight with concentration, hands moving delicately through a nest of wires.

"As long as you need." I move toward the terminal entrance,

positioning myself where I can see outside while still covering her position. "Don't rush. Do it right."

Through the terminal's grimy windows, lights approach—a vehicle moving fast, too fast for someone who's supposed to stop at the perimeter. Guardian HRS operators are positioning to intercept, but the vehicle swerves around their roadblock and heads directly for the terminal building.

"Vehicle in pursuit, attempting to ram the perimeter," comes over the radio.

"Engage." Confirmation comes over the comms from command

I raise my weapon, sighting on the approaching vehicle.

Guardian operators open fire, controlled bursts aimed at the engine and tires. The vehicle—a port authority utility truck—swerves violently but keeps coming. The driver is committed and willing to take rounds to reach the terminal. That level of dedication means true believer, fanatic, someone who'll die to complete Greer's plan.

The truck crashes through a chain-link fence, momentum carrying it into the terminal parking area. The driver's door opens before the vehicle fully stops, and a figure emerges firing a rifle. I return fire immediately, three controlled pairs center mass, and see the figure stumble but stay up.

Body armor, same as the shooters in the wilderness.

"Hostile in the terminal yard," I broadcast. "Armed and armored, moving toward the building."

I shift position to get a better angle, and something tears in my chest—not the ribs themselves but the soft tissue around them. Hot pain lances through me, but I keep firing. Two more rounds, and the hostile goes down.

This time, he goes down, rifle skittering across asphalt.

Movement to my left—a second figure, moving fast through the shadows. I track them, but my breathing is getting harder, each inhalation like knives in my chest. The compression wrap is helping but not enough. I squeeze the trigger, and the hostile drops.

They were in the truck too, using the driver as a distraction while they flanked around. Classic two-man assault, and I fell for it.

"Hostiles neutralized," I manage into the radio, though my voice sounds strained even to me. "Continuing security."

Carolina's voice cuts through the radio chatter, sharp with fear. "Flint—"

"I'm okay. Stay on the device. Don't look at me, don't stop working."

Operators flood into the terminal area, securing the fallen hostiles, checking for additional threats.

Carolina hasn't looked away from the device, hasn't let the firefight behind her break her concentration. That kind of focus is remarkable, the ability to maintain precision while chaos erupts around her.

But I can see the cost in the set of her shoulders, the too-fast rhythm of her breathing. She's running on adrenaline and determination, and both of those resources are finite.

"Talk to me, Carolina," I call, trying to keep my voice steady despite the increasing difficulty breathing. "Where are we?"

"Almost there." Her voice is tight. "I've bypassed the secondary circuits and disabled the remote trigger. Just the primary left, and it's..." She trails off, studying something intently. "It's different from the others. He's changed the configuration."

"Can you adapt?"

"I'm trying to." Her hands move, tracing wires, testing connections. "But there's something here I don't understand. A component that doesn't fit the pattern. It could be a decoy, or it could be the key to everything."

I watch her work, seeing the doubt creeping in. She's been brilliant all night, outthinking Greer at every turn, but exhaustion and fear are eroding her confidence. And Greer knows her well enough to exploit that—to plant doubt, to make her second-guess, to turn her greatest strength into a vulnerability.

"You're smarter than him," I say, pitching my voice to carry to her without being loud enough to startle. "You've always been smarter. That's why he resented you, why he's doing all this. Because he could never accept that you were better."

She glances back at me briefly, with fear in her eyes. "What if I'm not? What if he finally found my blind spot?"

"Then trust yourself anyway. Trust your training, your instincts, everything that makes you Carolina Sutton—the best EOD instructor the Army ever had, the woman who designed a system so good it took three years and obsessive planning to weaponize." I hold her gaze. "You've got this. I know you do."

She holds my eyes for a long moment, drawing strength from somewhere—my words, or her own reserves, or the simple fact that someone believes in her absolutely. Then she turns back to the device, and her shoulders settle. Her hands steady.

"Okay," she murmurs. "Okay. I see it now."

Her hands move with renewed confidence, choosing a path through the circuitry that looks random but must make sense to her understanding of Greer's psychology. She makes three cuts in rapid succession, each one deliberate, and then reaches for a bypass connection I don't understand.

"This is it," she says. "If I'm right, this disables the primary trigger. If I'm wrong..."

She doesn't finish the sentence. Doesn't need to. We both know what wrong means.

She makes the final connection, and for a heartbeat, nothing happens. Then the timer display flickers and goes dark. The device powers down, components going inert one by one, and Carolina sits back with a gasp that's half sob.

"It's done," she says, voice shaking. "It's done. Device Four is disarmed."

Relief crashes over me so intensely it's almost painful. She did it. We did it. Every device is neutralized, Greer's plan is defeated, and we're both still alive to see it.

FBI and bomb squad personnel flood into the terminal, but I only have eyes for Carolina, who's turned around and is crawling toward where I'm propped against a support pillar, her face wet with tears.

She reaches me and her hands go immediately to my chest,

seeing the way I'm breathing, the sweat on my face. "Oh God, Flint. Your ribs—you're hurt worse. I should have—"

"I'm okay." I catch her hands. "You did it. It's over."

She's shaking, adrenaline crash hitting hard, and I wrap my arms around her as best I can with the pain in my chest. We stay like that, both of us breathing—her easily, me with increasing difficulty—both of us alive.

She pulls back just enough to look at me, her hands framing my face, thumbs brushing across my cheekbones. Her eyes search mine—checking that I'm really here, really okay—and what I see in them makes my breath catch. Fear, yes, and relief, but also something deeper. Something that looks like what I'm feeling.

"I thought I lost you," she whispers, voice cracking.

"I'm here." I turn my head to press a kiss to her palm, then another to her wrist, feeling her pulse flutter against my lips. "I'm here, Carolina. We both are."

She makes a sound that's half laugh, half sob, and then she's kissing me. Not the desperate, hungry kiss from before—this one is softer, slower, thorough. Like she's trying to memorize the taste of me, the feel of my mouth against hers, proof that we're both alive and whole and together.

I kiss her back despite the pain, despite the blood loss trying to drag me under, despite the fact that we have an audience of FBI agents and Guardian operators. None of it matters. All that matters is her mouth on mine, her hands gentle on my face, the way she's holding me like I'm something precious.

When she finally pulls back, we're both breathing hard. She rests her forehead against mine, and I can feel tears on her cheeks—or maybe they're mine. Hard to tell anymore.

"Don't do that to me again," she says fiercely. "Don't almost die on me. I can't... I can't lose anyone else."

"Not planning on it." My hand comes up to tangle in her hair, and I pull her down for one more kiss—brief but intense. "But Carolina? Worth it. You were worth it."

The thing we're going to figure out, after we survive.

"You did it," I murmur, the words barely making it past the roughness in my throat.

Carolina's eyes find mine, wide and shining in the dim light. Relief. Shock. Something else simmers beneath the surface—something that feels like gravity pulling us together.

"Flint," she whispers, voice trembling.

The world tilts, the ache in my body drowned beneath a different kind of heat.

Our mouths meet—hard, hungry, every ounce of fear and relief and unspoken want igniting at once.

Her fingers clutch my vest, pulling me closer instead of pushing me away. She tastes like salt and tears and survival, the kiss rough-edged and breathless, desperate to make sure we're still here, still real.

When it finally breaks, she's still holding on, foreheads pressed together, breaths colliding in the space between us. The world is quiet except for our breathing and the echo of what just happened.

"I couldn't have done this without you." Her hand slips up to cup my face, thumb brushing the line of my cheek. Her voice shakes.

"Yes, you could have." But I turn my head to press a kiss to her palm. "But I'm glad you didn't have to.

Her breath hitches, and she's opening her mouth to respond when medical personnel with a stretcher arrive. They check my vitals, and one of them—Jenkins—frowns at what he finds.

"Possible pneumothorax developing," he says to his partner. "We need to transport immediately."

They load me onto the stretcher despite my protests that I can walk. Carolina stays close, her hand finding mine, and that touch is the last thing I'm aware of before the pain medication they push pulls me under.

ELEVEN

CAROLINA

THE HOSPITAL WAITING ROOM IS ANTISEPTIC AND FLUORESCENT, designed for efficiency rather than comfort.

I've been here for three hours while they work on Flint—monitoring the pneumothorax, ensuring his collapsed lung has fully reexpanded, checking for internal bleeding from the multiple vest impacts, all the medical intervention required when someone pushes through catastrophic chest trauma through sheer stubbornness and refuses to quit until the mission's done.

Agent Parker sits with me, nursing terrible vending machine coffee and occasionally trying to get me to eat something from the collection of snacks she's accumulated.

I can't.

My stomach is in knots, my mind replaying every moment from the terminal—the device, the firefight, Flint taking those rounds to his vest and still returning fire, the way his breathing got more labored as he maintained security while I worked.

I press my palms against my eyes, trying to stop the images, but they keep coming: the way he looked at me when he said I was worth it. The feel of his mouth on mine. The absolute certainty in his voice when he promised to keep me safe. The way he was struggling to breathe, but wouldn't leave his post.

"Ms. Sutton?" Parker's voice is gentle. "He's going to be fine."

"You don't know that." My voice is rougher than I intend. "He's being treated for a pneumothorax because of me. Because he kept throwing himself between me and danger, kept fighting when he should have been evacuated, kept—"

I stop, throat closing up. Kept looking at me like I mattered more than his own survival.

The truth is, I'm terrified. Not just of losing him to complications or respiratory failure. I'm terrified of how much I already feel for a man I've known less than forty-eight hours. Terrified of how right it felt to kiss him, to hold him, to promise we'd figure out what this is between us.

I'm terrified because I haven't felt this way since before Noah Parker died, since before I convinced myself that caring about people was just another way to fail them. And now here's Flint Morrison—stubborn, brave, ridiculous Flint—making me feel things I thought I'd buried for good.

Making me want things. Making me hope.

"I barely know him," I say quietly, more to myself than Parker.

"Sometimes that doesn't matter." Parker sets down her coffee. "Sometimes you just know."

I look at her, seeing understanding in her eyes. "Is it always this terrifying?"

"If it's real? Always." She offers a slight smile. "But that's how you know it's worth it."

He took multiple rounds to his vest for me. Fought with cracked ribs and a developing pneumothorax. Nearly suffocated maintaining security so I could focus on disarming a bomb. And I didn't even realize how bad it was until Device Four was neutralized and I turned to find him propped against a pillar, pale and gasping for air.

"He's going to be okay," Parker says for maybe the fifth time. "The doctor said the pneumothorax has been successfully treated, no permanent damage. The ribs will heal. He'll be on medical leave for a while, but he'll make a full recovery."

"He shouldn't have been out there at all," I say, voice rough from exhaustion and unshed tears. "He should have been in a hospital after the wilderness ambush. But he insisted on staying with me, on being my protection, and now..."

"And now he's alive because he's tough as hell, and you're alive because he was there." Parker sets down her coffee and turns to face me directly. "Ms. Sutton—Caro—what you and Morrison did tonight was extraordinary. Two devices disarmed, Greer's entire network dismantled, and minimal casualties despite multiple engagements. That doesn't happen without exceptional skill and courage from both of you."

I want to feel pride in that. Want to accept the praise and let it ease some of the guilt I've carried for three years. But all I can think about is Flint and the fact that he put himself between me and danger over and over because I designed a weapon that turned into a nightmare.

"He's stable."

I look up to see a doctor in scrubs, looking tired but satisfied.

"Mr. Morrison's pneumothorax has been successfully treated. We've inserted a chest tube to ensure complete lung re-expansion, and he's breathing much better. Three cracked ribs, extensive bruising, but no internal organ damage. He's going to need several weeks of recovery, but barring complications, he should heal completely."

Relief crashes over me so intensely I actually feel lightheaded. "Can I see him?"

"He's in room 314. He's on pain medication but awake, if you want to sit with him."

I'm moving before Parker can say anything, following the doctor through hospital corridors that blur together in my exhaustion.

Room 314 is private and quiet, monitors beeping softly, and there's Flint—propped up in bed to help his breathing, chest wrapped in bandages, a small drainage tube visible under the sheets. But his eyes are open, tracking me when I enter.

The sight of him stops me in the doorway. He looks wrong like this—too still, too pale, attached to oxygen. This is a man who threw himself into harm's way repeatedly, who fought through pain that would have dropped most people. Seeing him in a hospital bed, connected to machines, makes something crack open in my chest.

I cross the room in three strides, my hands reaching for him before I can think better of it. One hand finds his face, cupping his jaw, thumb brushing over his cheekbone. The other reaches for his hand, threading our fingers together, needing the physical confirmation that he's warm, alive, here.

His skin is cooler than normal, but his eyes are clear when they meet mine, and the smile that curves his mouth is small but real.

"Hey," he manages, and the sound of his voice—rough with anesthesia but unmistakably him—nearly undoes me.

"Hey yourself." My voice cracks embarrassingly. I don't care. "You scared the hell out of me."

"Sorry." His thumb moves weakly against my hand. "Didn't mean to."

"You couldn't breathe. You had a pneumothorax, and you just kept going like it was nothing."

"Not nothing," he admits, wincing slightly as he shifts. "Hurt like hell. But you needed me functional, so I stayed functional."

I want to yell at him. Want to tell him he's an idiot for pushing so hard, for staying when he should have gone, for risking everything to protect me. But what comes out instead is: "Thank you. For everything. For saving my life. Multiple times."

"Hey," he says, eyes focusing on mine despite the pain medication. "Are you okay?"

Of course, that's what he'd ask, even drugged and recovering from chest trauma. Not 'how bad are my injuries' or 'what happened'—but checking on me.

"I'm fine." I sit carefully on the edge of his bed, mindful of the chest tube and monitoring equipment. "You're the one who needed emergency treatment."

"But you disarmed the devices." There's pride in his voice, unmistakable even through the drug haze. "Beat Greer at his own game. Saved lives. Won."

"We won," I correct gently. "I couldn't have done it without you."

"Maybe. But you were always going to succeed. I just... made sure you got the chance." His eyes are trying to focus on my face, but keep drifting. "Worth it. You're worth it."

My throat closes up. I bring his hand to my cheek. "You almost died for me. Multiple times. That's not okay, Flint. That's not just doing your job."

"I know." His thumb moves weakly against my skin. "Told you before. Couldn't let... couldn't let anything happen to you."

"I care about you," I admit, the words easier than I expected. "And that's terrifying, because we just met, and this is probably just trauma bonding, and I don't know how to—"

"Doesn't matter." His eyes meet mine with surprising clarity, given the drugs. "Real or not, it's worth exploring. After I heal. We figure it out. Deal?"

"Deal." I lean down carefully and press a kiss to his forehead. "Sleep now. Heal. I'll be here when you wake up."

"Promise?"

"Promise."

His eyes drift closed, breath evening out into the rhythm of medicated sleep. I sit with him for a long time, holding his hand, watching the monitors that confirm he's breathing easily now, oxygen levels normal. The paracord bracelet is still on his wrist, blood-stained and battered.

Eventually, Parker finds me and gently insists I need rest, too. I have a hotel room waiting—a bed I haven't seen in over thirty hours —but I'm reluctant to leave. Only the promise that they'll call if anything changes convinces me to go, and even then, I extract Flint's promise that I'll be back first thing in the morning.

Three days later, I'm back at Guardian HRS facility, this time not as a consultant in crisis but as someone considering a future I didn't know I wanted until recently.

CJ's office looks the same—maps, monitors, the organized efficiency of a man who runs multiple teams across complicated operations. But the weight feels different now. I'm not here because the world is burning. I'm here because maybe I belong here.

"The FBI has formally closed the case on Marcus Greer," CJ

says, sliding a file across his desk toward me. "All devices accounted for and disarmed, his network dismantled, prosecution moving forward. They're recommending federal terrorism charges that will put him away for the rest of his life."

I scan the file, seeing photos of Greer in handcuffs, his expression no longer smug but defeated. He failed. His elaborate revenge plot, three years in the making, ended with me alive and his bombs disabled. Part of me wishes I could feel satisfaction in that.

Mostly, I just feel tired.

"How are you doing?" CJ asks, his voice gentler than I'd expect from someone with his reputation.

"Processing." It's the most honest answer I have. "Three days of sleep helped. So did hearing that none of Greer's people survived to try again. But I keep replaying everything, wondering what I missed, how I could have prevented—"

"You can't prevent someone else's choices to pursue revenge." CJ leans back in his chair. "You designed something innovative for training purposes. Greer corrupted it and used it to hurt people. That's on him, not you."

Intellectually, I know he's right. Emotionally, it'll take longer to believe it. But having survived Greer's test, having proven I could disarm devices specifically designed to kill me—that helps.

It doesn't erase the guilt about Noah Parker, but it adds something else to the equation. Evidence that I'm not a fraud, not a danger, not someone who should hide from her own expertise.

"Agent Parker mentioned you might have a proposition for me," I say, changing the subject slightly.

"We do." CJ pulls up something on his tablet, then turns it to face me. "Guardian HRS has been discussing expanding our capabilities to include EOD consultation and training. After watching you these past few days, we'd like you to join us. Contract basis initially, with the possibility of permanent hire if it's a good fit."

I study the details he's showing me—salary figures that make my wilderness guide work look like hobby income, benefits, flexible scheduling, and the chance to use my skills for something meaningful. Teaching Guardian operators advanced EOD techniques, consulting on device threats, maybe even developing new training protocols that honor what I learned from Noah's death without running from it.

"Would I be working with Flint's team?" I ask, trying to sound casual.

CJ's expression suggests I'm not fooling him. "Not directly—you'd be a contractor available to all Guardian teams. But Morrison will be on medical leave for at least four weeks while his ribs heal. Desk duty after that." He pauses meaningfully. "Though I imagine he'll be more amenable to recovery if someone he cares about is around the facility regularly."

"Is this a professional offer or a matchmaking attempt?"

"Can't it be both?" There's almost a smile in CJ's eyes. "Look, Sutton what you and Morrison did out there was remarkable. Not just the tactical success, but the way you worked together. Trust under pressure like that is rare. Whether that translates to something beyond the professional is your business. But Guardian HRS values people who can function in crisis, who have specialized skills, and who've proven they'll see a mission through regardless of personal cost. You check all those boxes."

I think about joining Guardian HRS, about building something new from the wreckage of my guilt and Greer's revenge. About being around Flint while he heals, while we figure out if what we feel is real or just adrenaline and proximity.

"I'll need to finish out my contract with Sierra Wilderness Expeditions," I say slowly. "Give them notice, train my replacement, do it right."

"We can work with that timeline."

"I'm not ready to make this decision. It feels simultaneously scary and right." I take a breath,

"Take some time," CJ leans back, "finish up with the guide company, and then we'll talk." He stands, signaling the meeting's end, but pauses at the door. "Morrison's in physical therapy right now, if you wanted to stop by. Room 108, east wing of Medical."

I head to room 108, where through the window I see Flint doing breathing exercises with a respiratory therapist. He's in Guardian

HRS athletic gear, moving carefully, obviously still in pain from the cracked ribs, but pushing through with determination.

The physical therapist sees me first and says something to Flint. He turns, face lighting up when he sees me—actual joy, unguarded and immediate. It does something to my chest, that expression, makes me think maybe this isn't just trauma bonding after all.

"Hey," he says, walking over carefully, one hand pressed lightly to his ribs. "What are you doing here?"

"Just had a meeting with CJ. Offered me a contract position." I watch his face carefully. "Teaching EOD, consulting on device threats, that kind of thing."

His smile grows. "Yeah? That's... that's good. Really good. We need someone with your expertise."

"And apparently, stubborn operators on medical leave need someone to make sure they don't push too hard in recovery." I gesture to where the therapist is watching. "CJ mentioned you'll be on restricted duty for a while."

"Four weeks minimum while these ribs heal. Then desk duty." He says it without regret. "Totally worth it, though."

"Idiot," I say, but there's no heat in it.

"Your idiot, if you want." He says it lightly, but there's a real question underneath. "We said we'd figure out what this is, after. It's after. So... what do you think?"

I step closer. "I think it might be real. I want to find out."

"Me too." His hand comes up to cup my face. "I'm not good at relationships. I'm gone a lot, the work is dangerous, and I carry baggage."

"I'm not great at them either. But maybe we're both ready to try something different."

"Different sounds good." He leans down slowly, giving me time to pull back if I want, but I don't. I meet him halfway, and the kiss is gentle, testing.

When we pull back, he's smiling. "So. We're doing this?"

"We're doing this." I step back. "But first, you finish recovery. I'll finish with my guide company. Let's do this right."

"Sounds like a plan. Dinner tonight? If you're still in town."

"Dinner sounds good."

I leave him to finish his session, but I can't quite stop smiling as I walk back through the Guardian HRS facility.

The future feels uncertain in ways that would have terrified me a week ago. But now, having survived Greer's worst and disarmed every device he built to destroy me, uncertainty feels like possibility instead of threat.

TWELVE

CAROLINA

ONE WEEK LATER

Flint's apartment is smaller than I expected—a one-bedroom in a secure building near Guardian HRS, furnished with the kind of functional minimalism that speaks to a man who's rarely home. But it's clean, organized, and the west-facing windows let in golden evening light that softens everything.

"You didn't have to come check on me." He's on the couch, breathing easier now though still moving carefully to protect his healing ribs. The worst of the bruising has faded from black and purple to greenish-yellow.

"You're bored and going stir-crazy," I counter, setting down the takeout I brought—Thai food from the place he mentioned liking. "And your physical therapist called me. Said you're pushing too hard, not resting enough."

"Traitor," he mutters, but there's warmth in his eyes when he looks at me.

"Doctor cleared me for light activity," he says, pulling me closer gently. "Ribs are healing well. No more breathing issues."

"Good." I curl into his side, careful of his chest. "Because I officially accepted CJ's offer today. I start next week."

His face lights up. "Yeah? You going to take it?"

"Yes."

His arms tighten around me carefully. "That's fantastic."

We eat in comfortable silence, then talk for hours about everything—my plans for the EOD program, his gradual return to duty, the future we're building.

When the conversation lulls, he turns to me with a serious expression.

"Carolina," he says, voice low. "I need you to know something. What I feel for you—it's not trauma bonding. It's real. You're brilliant, brave, beautiful, and I'm falling for you more every day."

My breath catches. "Flint..."

"You don't have to say it back. I just needed you to know."

"We barely know each other."

"You disarm bombs while staying calmer than most people order coffee. You're brave enough to face your worst nightmare because people need you. You look at me like I matter—not just as a Guardian, but as a person." His thumb traces my cheekbone. "And I want to keep discovering everything else."

I silence him with a kiss, pouring everything I feel into it. When we break apart, we're both breathing carefully—him because of his ribs, me because of emotion.

The kiss starts slow, testing what his healing ribs can handle. But heat builds quickly—a week of careful distance, suppressed want, the bone-deep need to confirm we're both alive and here.

His hands slide into my hair, angling my head. I respond carefully, palms flat against his chest, feeling his heartbeat but being gentle with the still-tender ribs.

The kiss turns hungry, desperate, all the fear and adrenaline of the past week transmuting into something hotter, more immediate.

"Carolina," he breathes against my mouth. "If we keep going..."

"I know." I pull back to meet his eyes. "I don't want to hurt you. Your ribs—"

"Are fine if we're careful." He kisses me again, slower but

deeper. "I need you. Need to feel you. Been thinking about it all week."

His answer isn't words—it's another kiss. Slower this time, but deeper, hotter, the kind that feels like surrender and promise all tangled together.

His hand slides to the back of my neck, drawing me closer until there's no space left to think, only the thud of his heartbeat against my chest and the taste of him stealing what's left of my breath.

His hands slide down my sides, thumbs brushing the strip of skin where my shirt has ridden up, and I arch into the touch.

We navigate his injury carefully—my hands gentle when they encounter bandages, our movements slow and deliberate. I end up straddling his lap, my hands framing his face as I kiss him deeply.

His hands span my waist, sliding up beneath my shirt, calloused palms rough against my skin. The sensation sends shivers through me, heat pooling low in my belly. When his fingers find the clasp of my bra, he pauses, giving me space to refuse.

I don't.

Instead, I pull back long enough to drag my shirt over my head, letting it fall to the floor beside the couch.

Flint's eyes go dark, pupils blown wide as he takes me in—half-naked in his lap, flushed and wanting.

"Beautiful," he murmurs, then leans forward to press kisses along my collarbone, my shoulder, the upper swell of my breast.

My head falls back, breath coming faster as his mouth explores. His hands are everywhere—spanning my ribs, tracing my spine, mapping every inch of exposed skin with a thoroughness that makes me tremble.

"Bedroom," I manage to gasp out, though the word feels ridiculous when every inch of me is on fire from his touch, his calloused hands sliding up my thighs like he owns them already. My skin tingles, heat pooling low in my belly, and I can barely think straight with the ache building between my legs.

"You're in charge of the pace," he says, hands spanning my waist. "But God, Carolina, I need you."

I lean in and kiss him fiercely, pouring all my pent-up need into it, my tongue tangling with his to silence any more hesitation.

He chuckles low, a predatory sound that vibrates against my lips. His hands are on my waist, firm, commanding, surprising me with his strength.

His fingers dig into my flesh like he's already mapping out how he'll take me apart.

"Get these off," he orders, voice low and rough, nodding toward his jeans with a tilt of his chin.

I fumble with his belt buckle, my hands trembling with anticipation, the metal clinking softly as I yank it open. The zipper follows, rasping down with a sound that echoes in the charged air, my pulse racing as I feel the heat radiating from him beneath the denim.

He lifts his hips just enough— a controlled, powerful motion despite the wince that flickers across his face—allowing me to shove the jeans and boxers down his legs.

His cock springs free, thick and hard, veins pulsing along its length, the tip already glistening with pre-cum.

God, it's bigger than I imagined during all those stolen glances on the trail, and the sight of it—standing proud for me—sends a fresh wave of heat throbbing between my legs. I'm immediately soaked as I stare, mesmerized.

My mouth waters, and my core clenches in anticipation. God, I've imagined this, fantasized about how he'd feel, but seeing him like this—vulnerable position, yet radiating control—it's intoxicating.

"Climb on and show me how much you want this," he says, his voice a gravelly command as he guides me over him, the head of his cock teasing my slick entrance.

I lower myself slowly, savoring the stretch as he fills me, inch by throbbing inch, a gasp escaping me at the exquisite burn. The sensation is overwhelming—full, perfect, like he was made for me. But even as I start to rock my hips, finding a rhythm, he takes over.

His hands lock onto my ass, dictating the pace, pulling me down harder onto him.

"Fuck, I've wanted my cock buried in this tight little pussy since I first glassed you on that ridge," he growls, eyes locked on mine, dark and possessive. "Watched you moving like that, all fire and curves, and all I could think was how I'd bend you over right there in the dirt, spread those legs wide, and slam into you deep and hard, owning every moan until you screamed my name for the whole damn valley to hear."

His hips buck as I bottom out on his cock.

"Or shove you down to your knees in the grass, gripping your hair to guide your mouth over my cock, making you take me all the way while I tell you how good you look choking on what belongs to me. Hell, I'd pin you hard against a tree, your palms flat on the bark as I thrust into you from behind, relentless and rough, claiming you so completely that you'd never forget who you belong to, coming undone only when I say so."

Heat floods my cheeks, but it's not embarrassment—it's arousal, pure and scorching, making me grind down harder on him, my slick walls fluttering at the vivid, commanding images he's painting.

God, he's been thinking about me like that? Filthy, dominant thoughts that match the wild man I glimpsed on that hike?

My thoughts scatter. It turns me on more than I expected, the way his words paint these raw, explicit pictures—me on my knees for him, his hands pinning me down, claiming every part of me. I moan, my nails digging into his shoulders, careful of his bandages, but he doesn't flinch.

Instead, he laughs again, that deep, rumbling sound that makes my walls flutter around him.

"I imagined our first time together as something far more vigorous than you riding me," he says, thrusting up into me with a sharp snap of his hips that hits deep, making stars burst behind my eyelids. "But I like this—watching you take me, your tits bouncing, that pretty face all flushed."

"God, don't stop talking like that," I gasp, my voice breathy and desperate, leaning down to nip at his jaw as I roll my hips in response, chasing the friction.

His words are like fuel to the fire already raging inside me, his filthy mind turning me on in ways I never expected—raw, unfiltered, and so damn possessive.

He grins up at me, that wicked, knowing flash of teeth that makes my pulse stutter, clearly encouraged by my plea, his eyes darkening with fresh heat as he tightens his grip on my ass.

"Been imagining pinning you against a tree, slamming into you from behind, feeling you clench around me while the wind whips around us. Or better yet, tying your hands with my belt, making you beg for every inch."

A soft moan escapes my lips at his words, the imagery searing into my brain—me helpless and wanting, at his mercy under the stars—and I can't help but grind down harder, taking him deeper, my inner walls pulsing around his thick length as slick heat coats us both.

"Yes... like that," I whisper, my voice husky with need, my nails digging into his shoulders as I ride him faster, the confession drawing me in even more, making me ache for the reality of his dominance.

He realizes it instantly, that hungry glint in his eyes sharpening as he watches my face contort in pleasure, feels the way I tighten around him, my body betraying just how much his raw talk turns me on.

It's written all over his expression—that smug, alpha satisfaction —as his hands slide up my back, one tangling in my hair while the other flexes on my hip, urging me on with a low, approving rumble in his chest.

"Fuck, you like that, don't you?" he murmurs, his voice a gravelly tease, testing the waters as his thumb brushes the edge of my hipbone, dipping toward where we're joined. "With my belt... I could loop it around your wrists, hold you steady while I fuck you senseless. Or wrap it once around your waist, yank you back onto me harder when you start to squirm, making sure you feel every thrust like it's yours to earn."

His words ignite me, each filthy fantasy stoking the fire in my veins. I ride him faster, chasing the building pressure, but he's still the one in charge—his thumb finds my clit, rubbing in firm circles that have me whimpering, his other hand in my hair, tugging my head back to expose my throat.

His words send a fresh wave of heat coiling low in my belly, the promise of restraint and control making my thighs tremble as I lift and slam down onto him again, the slick sounds of our bodies meeting filling the air.

"More," I breathe out, almost a plea, my head falling back as pleasure builds, his thickness stretching me perfectly, hitting that spot inside that makes my vision blur.

I love how he's pushing these boundaries, his voice wrapping around me like a command I can't resist.

He chuckles darkly, the sound vibrating through his chest and into me, his free hand coming up to cup my breast, thumb circling my nipple roughly before pinching just hard enough to draw a gasp from my lips.

"Greedy girl," he rasps, his eyes devouring the way I arch into his touch.

My rhythm falters as a whine slips free, my body on fire with the need to submit to every filthy scenario he's weaving.

"That's it," he murmurs, voice laced with heat. "Show me how wet you get for these thoughts. I've pictured your mouth on me too —sucking me deep while I tell you exactly how I'd ruin you. Come on, baby, let go. Soak my cock like I've dreamed."

The command shatters me. Pleasure coils tight and snaps, my orgasm crashing over me in waves, my body shuddering as I cry out, clenching around him.

He groans, hips bucking once more before he follows, spilling hot inside me with a satisfied curse, his grip bruising as he holds me in place through every pulse.

Afterward, we're tangled together on his couch, my head on his chest, rising and falling with his steady breaths. His fingers trace lazy, possessive patterns on my bare shoulder, a reminder that even spent, he's the one who calls the shots.

The sun has set, leaving the apartment in blue twilight, but neither of us moves to turn on the lights—content in the afterglow of his unshakeable control.

"You liked all that, didn't you?" he says after a long, quiet stretch, his voice low and rumbling against my ear, that smug edge creeping back in as his hand slides down to rest on the curve of my hip. "Fuck, baby, the way you clenched around me... You were soaking just from the words."

Heat blooms fresh in my cheeks, but I don't deny it—can't, not when my body still hums with the echoes of those fantasies, my pulse quickening at the mere reminder. I tilt my head up, meeting his gaze in the dim light, my voice soft but honest.

"Yeah... It was hot, the way you said it—like you meant every word."

"I meant every word," he replies, his tone dropping even lower, laced with that raw intent that sends a shiver racing down my spine. "I like to fuck, baby—and I like it hot, spicy, and edgy. No holding back, no vanilla bullshit. And I very much like being in charge, calling the shots, watching you unravel because of it."

His eyes darken as he speaks, that predatory spark flaring to life, and I feel it before I see it: his cock twitching against my thigh, hardening steadily, thick and insistent as it presses into my skin.

He shifts slightly, his grip tightening on my hip, pulling me closer so I can't ignore the growing heat of him.

A thrill shoots through me at his command, that unyielding tone wrapping around my will like a vice, making resistance impossible— and the truth is, I don't want to resist.

My body moves before my mind catches up, sliding off the couch with a soft rustle of the sheet, sinking to my knees on the cool hardwood floor between his spread thighs. The twilight casts shadows over his form, highlighting the flex of his muscles as he sits back, watching me with that intense gaze, his cock now fully hard and curving upward, flushed and ready.

I lean in, my hands sliding up his thighs to steady myself, fingers brushing the base of him as I part my lips and take him in—slow at first, tongue swirling around the thick head, tasting the salt of his arousal mixed with the remnants of us.

He groans low, one hand coming to rest on the back of my head, not forcing but guiding, fingers threading through my hair as I hollow my cheeks and sink deeper, sucking with a rhythm that's all for him, all to prove how those words ignited something wild in me.

The sounds he makes—rough, approving—spur me on, my own heat building again as I bob my head, taking him to the back of my throat, gagging just a little before pulling back to tease the underside with flicks of my tongue.

"Fuck, yes," he mutters, hips bucking slightly into my mouth, his grip tightening as he watches through hooded eyes. "Just like that— my good girl, showing me what you can handle."

I lose myself in it, the power in his pleasure, until his breaths turn ragged, his body tensing, and with a final, deep thrust against my tongue, he comes hard, spilling into my mouth in hot pulses that I swallow greedily, milking him through it until he's shuddering and spent.

When he finally pulls me up, his touch gentler now, I curl back against him on the couch, both of us boneless and sated once more, the air thick with the scent of sex and satisfaction. His arm drapes over me possessively, our breaths syncing in the quiet.

"So," he says, voice rough with satisfaction and exhaustion, "does this influence your decision about the Guardian HRS job?"

I prop myself up to look at him, taking in his tousled hair, the satisfied smile playing at his mouth, the way he's looking at me like I'm something precious.

"I'm definitely going to take it now."

His smile widens. "Yeah?"

"Yeah." I gesture between us, "I want to see where it goes."

He pulls me down for a kiss that's gentle and sweet and full of promise, his lips lingering like he's sealing the deal.

We stay like that for hours, talking quietly, stealing kisses, learning each other's bodies now that we have time and safety to explore. And when I eventually need to leave—early meeting with CJ to finalize my contract—Flint walks me to the door, kisses me goodbye with enough heat to make me consider canceling my morning plans, and extracts a promise that I'll come back tomorrow.

"Every day if you want," I tell him, meaning it.

"I very much want," he says, and watches me leave with eyes that promise he's already counting the hours until I return.

THREE MONTHS LATER

The Guardian HRS training facility is empty except for me and the advanced EOD operators I've been training over the past six weeks. We're in the final session of the course I designed—practical application using adaptive triggers in scenarios that push their skills without putting them in actual danger.

It's the culmination of everything I learned from Noah Parker's death, from Greer's weaponization, from my own journey back to trusting my expertise.

I watch as the last operator completes the disarmament sequence, steady hands and clear thinking under simulated pressure. When the device powers down successfully, a swell of pride overcomes me. This is what I was meant to do—not run from my past, but transform it into something that saves lives.

"Well done," I tell the group as they gather for debrief. "You've all passed this level of certification. The skills you've learned here will make you among the best EOD operators in the country. Stay humble, and never assume you know everything about a device just because you've seen one like it before."

They file out, chatting among themselves, and I'm packing up my equipment when I sense Flint before I see him.

"How'd it go?" he asks, moving into the room.

"Perfect. They're all certified." I close my equipment case and turn to face him fully. "How was your day?"

"Boring desk work and planning. CJ is making noises about clearing me for light fieldwork next month." He stops in front of me, close enough to touch. "But that's not what I came to talk about."

"Oh?"

He pulls something from his pocket—a paracord bracelet, new and clean, woven in green and tan to match the one on his wrist. "I made you something. Thought maybe... if you wanted... we could carry the same reminder."

I take the bracelet carefully, feeling the texture of the weave, understanding what he's offering. His bracelet represents promises, failure, and loss. This new one—woven for me—represents promises, too, as well as survival, partnership, and the fact that sometimes you get there in time and everyone makes it out alive.

"It's perfect," I say, and hold out my wrist so he can tie it on. His fingers are deft, and when he's done, the bracelet sits comfortably against my skin, weighted with meaning.

"Partners," he says simply. "In work and... everything else. If you still want that."

For three months, we've been figuring this out—dinners, conversations, building trust that goes beyond trauma bonding—learning each other outside of crisis, discovering that what we felt in those desperate hours was real and lasting. It hasn't been perfect or easy, but it's been genuine.

"I still want that," I tell him, and pull him down for a kiss that's become familiar but never routine. "Partners in everything."

When we pull apart, he's smiling, and I'm smiling too—real joy, earned through survival and healing and choosing to trust again. The past doesn't disappear, the ghosts don't stop haunting, but they don't have to control the future either.

We walk out of the training facility together, his hand finding mine, both of us wearing bracelets that remind us what matters. Outside, the California sun is setting over Guardian HRS, casting everything in a golden and amber light.

Somewhere, Marcus Greer is in federal prison, his revenge plot defeated, his genius turned to nothing by the woman he tried to break. Somewhere, Private Noah Parker's memory is honored not by my guilt but by the lives I save teaching others to survive. And here, right now, I'm whole in ways I didn't think possible three months ago.

Flint squeezes my hand, and I squeeze back. We survived. We healed. And now we're building something new together—something that honors the past without being trapped by it, something that feels like home.

"Dinner at my place?" he asks. "I'm cooking, not ordering takeout for once."

"What are you making?"

"Not telling. You'll have to come find out."

"Mystery dinner. Risky proposition."

"You handle bombs for a living. I think you can handle my cooking." He grins at me, and I see the man who tracked me through the wilderness, who took bullets to keep me safe, who believed in me when I didn't believe in myself. And I see the man I'm choosing every day, not because trauma bonded us but because he's worth choosing.

"Okay," I agree. "Mystery dinner it is."

We walk toward the parking lot together as the sun dips below the horizon, two people who found each other in the worst circumstances and built something lasting from it. The future stretches ahead, uncertain and full of possibility, and for the first time in three years, I'm not afraid of it.

I'm ready.

AUTHOR'S NOTE:
Thank you for reading FLINT!

IF YOU'RE CRAVING MORE HIGH-STAKES MISSIONS, MORALLY GRAY operators, and romance forged in gunfire—I've got you covered.

Read the next Guardian HRS Short Read: HAWK → Read Here!

BINGE THE GUARDIAN HOSTAGE RESCUE SPECIALISTS (HRS) WORLD NOW

. . .

The Guardian HRS universe is MASSIVE, and multiple complete series are waiting for you:

GUARDIAN HRS CORE SERIES - *Complete and ready to binge* **Alpha, Bravo, Charlie,** and **Delta** teams handling the extractions governments won't touch. These operators live in the shadows, fight in the dark, and fall hard for the women who make them want to step into the light.
- Elite hostage rescue specialists
- International black ops missions
- Brothers-in-arms who become family
- The women tough enough to love them

Start with Alpha Team, Book 1 → Rescuing Zoe → READ HERE

CERBERUS PERSONAL SECURITY SERIES -*GHOST*, *BRASS*, and Whisper, *with more coming soon.*

The CERBERUS series is Guardian HRS Adjacent - Grittier, Darker, More Possessive

When Guardian HRS needs someone protected but the threat level is DEFCON 1, they call Cerberus. These aren't your typical bodyguards—they're the operators who live between protection and elimination. More alpha. More possessive. More willing to cross lines the Guardians won't.

Think: Dominant protector heroes who'll burn the world down to keep their woman safe.
- Close protection with deadly force authorized
- Operators who don't play by the rules
- Obsessive, possessive, "mine to protect" romance

• Higher heat, darker themes

START WITH GHOST → READ HERE

CAN'T DECIDE? WANT IT ALL?
→ Read Guardian HRS first (it's the foundation), then dive into Cerberus for the grittier adjacent operations.

THE GUARDIAN HRS PROMISE:

Every book features:

☑ Competent, dangerous heroes with hidden depths

☑ Strong heroines who don't need saving (but get protected anyway)

☑ Found family and brotherhood

☑ Realistic tactical operations (I do my research)

☑ Romance that earns the HEA

☑ Standalone books with interconnected world

DON'T WAIT - START YOUR BINGE NOW

A PERSONAL INVITATION

Flint and Carolina's story is a 35,000 word **novella**—just a taste and a quick, intense introduction to the Guardian HRS world. But here's what you need to know: **nearly every other book in this universe is a massive, extra-long novel.**

We're talking 80,000-100,000+ words of:
- Complex multi-layered missions
- Deep character development
- Multiple POVs and subplots
- Extended tactical operations
- Slow-burn romance that EARNS the payoff
- Brotherhood dynamics and found family

FLINT gave you a taste.
The full series gives you a FEAST.

Think of this novella as your amuse-bouche—a carefully crafted bite designed to show you what I'm capable of.

. . .

THE MAIN GUARDIAN HRS AND CERBERUS BOOKS? THOSE ARE five-course meals. Beefy, satisfying, the kind of novels you lose an entire weekend to because you physically cannot put them down.

IF FLINT AND CARLOINA'S STORY RESONATED WITH YOU IN JUST 35,000 words—imagine what I can do with **three times the page count.**

THE FULL-LENGTH NOVELS DIVE DEEP:
- Operators with complex trauma and layered backstories
- Missions that span multiple countries and weeks of operations
- Romance that develops over hundreds of pages (not hours)
- Secondary characters who become your new obsessions
- Plot twists that will make you gasp at 2 AM
- Action sequences that feel like watching a movie

The Guardian HRS world is waiting.
Your next operator is loading his weapon.
And you've got 30+ extra-long novels ready to devour.

WHICH TEAM WILL YOU CHOOSE?

STAY DANGEROUS,

Ellie Masters

 **START BINGING NOW**

**Guardian HRS Alpha Team, Book 1: RESCUING ZOE →
CLICK HERE**

Cerberus Book 1: GHOST → CLICK HERE

The Guardian HRS world has **30+** complete books waiting for you. Operators are falling in love. Missions are launching. And somewhere in this universe, your next *book boyfriend* is loading his weapon and preparing to risk everything for the woman who makes him feel human again.

🎯 READY FOR YOUR NEXT MISSION?

ELLZ BELLZ

ELLIE'S FACEBOOK READER GROUP

If you are interested in joining the **ELLZ BELLZ**, Ellie's Facebook reader group, we'd love to have you.

Join Ellie's **ELLZ BELLZ**.
The **ELLZ BELLZ** Facebook Reader Group

Sign up for Ellie's Newsletter.
Elliemasters.com/newslettersignup

Rescuing Angie

Rescuing Isabelle

Rescuing Carmen

Rescuing Rosalie

Rescuing Kaye

Cara's Protector

Rescuing Barbi

Charlie Team

Rescuing Rebel

Rescuing Stitch

Rescuing Mia

Jenna's Protector

Rescuing Sophia

Rescuing Malia

Rescuing Ally (Part 1)

Rescuing Ally (Part 2)

Delta Team

Rescuing Ember

Rescuing Aria

STANDALONES IN THE GUARDIAN HOSTAGE RESCUE SERIES YOU CAN READ ANYTIME

Military Romance

Guardian Personal Protection Specialists

Sybil's Protector

Lyra's Protector

Angel's Peak Series
Steamy Instalove Small Town

Brody

Cage

Billionaire Romance

Billionaire Boys Club

Hawke

Richard

Contemporary Romance

Cocky Captain

Romantic Suspense

EACH BOOK IS A STANDALONE NOVEL.

The Starling

The Swan

~AND~

Science Fiction

Ellie Masters writing as L.A. Warren
Vendel Rising: a Science Fiction Serialized Novel

**If you enjoyed this book by Ellie Masters, the LIGHTER SIDE of
the Jet & Ellie writing duo, and aren't afraid of edgier writing,
you might enjoy reading BDSM themed books written by Jet, the
DARKER SIDE of the Masters' Writing Team.**

The DARKER SIDE

Jet Masters is the darker side of the Jet & Ellie writing duo!

Romantic Suspense

Changing Roles Series:

THIS SERIES MUST BE READ IN ORDER.

Command Me

Control Me

Collar Me

Embracing FATE

Seizing FATE

Accepting FATE

HOT READS

A STANDALONE NOVEL.

Down the Rabbit Hole

Light BDSM Romance

The Ties that Bind

EACH BOOK IN THIS SERIES CAN BE READ AS A STANDALONE AND IS ABOUT A DIFFERENT COUPLE WITH AN HEA.

Alexa

Penny

Michelle

Ivy

HOT READS

Becoming His Series

THIS SERIES MUST BE READ IN ORDER.

The Ballet

Learning to Breathe

Becoming His

Dark Captive Romance

A STANDALONE NOVEL.

She's MINE

About the Author

Ellie Masters is a USA Today Bestselling author and Amazon Top 15 Author who writes Angsty, Steamy, Heart-Stopping, Pulse-Pounding, Can't-Stop-Reading Romantic Suspense. In addition, she's a wife, military mom, doctor, and retired Colonel. She writes romantic suspense filled with all your sexy, swoon-worthy alpha men. Her writing will tug at your heartstrings and leave your heart racing.

Born in the South, raised under the Hawaiian sun, Ellie has traveled the globe while in service to her country. The love of her life, her amazing husband, is her number one fan and biggest supporter. And yes! He's read every word she's written.

She has lived all over the United States—east, west, north, south and central—but grew up under the Hawaiian sun. She's also been privileged to have lived overseas, experiencing other cultures and making lifelong friends. Now, Ellie is proud to call herself a Southern transplant, learning to say y'all and "bless her heart" with the best of them.

Ellie's favorite way to spend an evening is curled up on a couch, laptop in place, watching a fire, drinking a good wine, and bringing forth all the characters from her mind to the page and hopefully into the hearts of her readers.

FOR MORE INFORMATION
elliemasters.com

Connect with Ellie Masters

Website:
elliemasters.com
Purchase Direct:
elliemasters.com/shopify
Amazon Author Page:
elliemasters.com/amazon
Facebook:
elliemasters.com/Facebook
Goodreads:
elliemasters.com/Goodreads
Bookbub:
elliemasters.com/Bookbub
Instagram:
elliemasters.com/Instagram

Final Thoughts

I hope you enjoyed this book as much as I enjoyed writing it. If you enjoyed reading this story, please consider leaving a review on Amazon and Goodreads, and please let other people know. A sentence is all it takes. Friend recommendations are the strongest catalyst for readers' purchase decisions! And I'd love to be able to continue bringing the characters and stories from My-Mind-to-the-Page.

Second, call or e-mail a friend and tell them about this book. If you really want them to read it, gift it to them. If you prefer digital friends, please use the "Recommend" feature of Goodreads to spread the word.

Or visit my blog https://elliemasters.com, where you can find out more about my writing process and personal life.

Come visit The EDGE: Dark Discussions where we'll have a chance to talk about my works, their creation, and maybe what the future has in store for my writing.

Facebook Reader Group: Ellz Bellz

Thank you so much for your support!

Love,

Ellie

Dedication

This book is dedicated to you, my reader. Thank you for spending a few hours of your time with me. I wouldn't be able to write without you to cheer me on. Your wonderful words, your support, and your willingness to join me on this journey is a gift beyond measure.

Whether this is the first book of mine you've read, or if you've been with me since the very beginning, thank you for believing in me as I bring these characters 'from my mind to the page and into your hearts.'

Love,
Ellie

THE END

www.ingramcontent.com/pod-product-compliance
Lightning Source LLC
Chambersburg PA
CBHW031958140726

47988CB00019B/2516